Love
in a
Scottish Storm

Veronika Sophia Robinson

Sweet Cinnamon
Romance

For the violinists in my family:
my maternal grandfather, Erwin,
and my daughter, Beth.

Veronika Robinson is an Australian author living in rural Cumbria, England, with her husband, Paul, and two black cats, Kali and Pelé, in a three-hundred-year-old cottage overlooking the Pennines. As a teenager, she devoured romance novels instead of biology textbooks, and was regularly given detention by her science teacher for drawing "the wrong sort of hearts!"

In her mid twenties, after kissing too many frogs, Veronika met her soul's love, Paul. It was at this time that she became a marriage celebrant. All these years later, she still writes and officiates beautiful wedding ceremonies. Although voted by her secondary-school teachers as the student most likely to fail in life, Veronika couldn't be happier with the way she spends her days.

A late bloomer, in her mid fifties she earned her Master's Degree in Creative Writing from the University of Cumbria despite no previous academic qualification. A prolific writer, her books span fiction and non-fiction.

Love in a Scottish Storm
© Veronika Sophia Robinson
© Cover illustration by Heidi Harbers
Published by Sweet Cinnamon Romance
An imprint of Starflower Press
ISBN: 978-1-7398336-9-5
St. Valentine's Day 2023

A CIP catalogue record for this book is available from the British Library.

Published by Sweet Cinnamon Romance, an imprint of Starflower Press www.starflowerpress.com

www.veronikarobinson.com

Sweet Cinnamon Romances
are contemporary love stories set around the world.
Cinnamon symbolises abundance, protection and passion.

The Storm

'Get out of this storm, lassie,' the irate postman yelled as he climbed back into his red van. 'It's not safe to be out. People have died in storms like this.'

Liesel smiled at him to acknowledge the weather, but she was more interested in the sense of déjà vu about this place, if that's what it was. The weather would have to wait for her, not the other way around.

'I will!' she promised, crossing her fingers at the deliberate lie, but as soon as he was out of sight she tied her chocolate-brown hair up into a pony tail, to secure it from the wind, and then wandered on through the rural village until she was past the school, post office and pub.

Liesel had been in the highlands of Scotland for just two days, and although it was her first visit, she felt as if she'd been here before. It was to be a short holiday... just a week. The irony was that she hadn't wanted to come here. No, not at all. Scotland was definitely not her choice of destination. But now she was here, there was something in her bones that told her she wouldn't leave in a hurry. More than once she laughed it off. It was a stupid thought. Maybe she'd just been travelling on her own for too long, and was trying to put off the inevitable: going back to her real life.

There were decisions to be made, and they weighed heavily on her heart. Why wasn't life simpler? she wondered.

Duncan's last words came to mind: 'You have to see the loch by Stoneyhill Castle. I'll meet you there, and we can spend a week together. Don't argue, Liesel. It'll do us both good.'

Of course, she'd tried arguing; had insisted that she wanted to be on her own, but eventually she surrendered.

Rugged up against the bitter winds, Liesel stopped to look at the signs flapping about on the village notice board. Nothing of interest. But…but there was something about the place, though, that she couldn't quite put her finger on. It didn't make sense. All she knew was that she was meant to be here; it was almost like a gravitational pull. Nothing she could see identified what the urgent feeling to stay was all about. Where was it coming from? The wind taunted her, carrying the message: *You know this place*.

A truck splashed water up from the road as it whizzed by, spraying her jeans. The driver stuck his head from the window, unapologetically, and yelled, 'Get out of the storm, gal! It'll kill you!'

Liesel told herself that she couldn't understand the thick accent, and waved him off.

Turning sideways, in the hope of feeling some inner strength against the howling gales, she rushed into the village shop to take refuge, and asked if there were any tourist places nearby of interest.

'Today? In this weather?'

The plump, middle-aged woman raised her eyebrows in disbelief, and giggled her way through a nervous laugh. 'Well, there's always the haunted castle up the hill, ma wee bonnie lass' she said. 'But of course, it's not open to the public. The residence is strictly private. It's a shame, though, because the views over the loch are beautiful. Not that you'd see anything today in this storm. Now dear, you best get out of here while you can. It's going to get a whole lot worse.'

'Why is it haunted?' Liesel asked, her curiosity

growing. Goosebumps settled on her neck as she shivered at the cold which had followed her through the front door.

'Isaac Heathfield's wife, the late Marylynn, flung herself down the stairs in a fit of rage, and died instantly.'

Liesel gasped. 'How awful! That's tragic. What happened to Isaac? How did he cope?'

'He still lives there, but he's a hermit. We hardly see him down the village. Very occasionally he drinks at the pub, but that's only if he's been away on business. He keeps on a few staff, but they've all signed a privacy policy, so they're sworn to secrecy. No one *really* knows what goes on up there. Everything about the castle and about his life is shrouded by the memory of that fateful day.'

The shopkeeper leant forward and whispered, despite Liesel being the only person in the shop: 'Word has it, though, that she comes back every night; her cries calling through the ancient hallways. It's said that he doesn't sleep at night; can't sleep at night. He's tormented by her howls.'

Liesel put her hand to her chest, as if to hold her wounded heart; as if his pain was her pain. 'How heartbreaking for him to lose someone he loved.'

'Oh, there was no love lost there! If he's grieving, it's because there'd be no heir to the family fortune. He's the last in the family line. Without an heir, that castle goes to the government. It's been in the same family for centuries. *Centuries!* Marylynn was handpicked for him by his late grandfather a long time ago. She was deeply in love with Isaac, but he didn't see it. Or, didn't want to see it. She gave up her life in Boston to be here. Marylynn was from a well-to-do family. Truth was, she could have had any man she wanted. Poor lass left all that behind to provide Isaac with his much-needed heir. I could never understand why. There's nothing for a woman up there on that hill. Not unless she thrives on isolation.'

'This is the saddest story I've ever heard.' Liesel wiped a tear from her eye.

'Rumour has it that Marylynn was pregnant.'

'He lost a wife *and* a baby?'

'Afraid so.'

'What does he do up there, all alone?'

Liesel just couldn't understand why he'd stay in the castle if he was in such pain. With heaviness weighing upon her heart, she just couldn't bear the thought of anyone going through such grief.

'Your guess is as good as mine.' The shopkeeper began dusting a shelf, then continued her conversation. 'Now, you can see the same loch from over near Iona Road. Take the first right after the pub, then travel for two miles, then take the left at the crossroad. That would be a nice place for you to visit, but I don't think you should go there today. This storm is going to get a whole lot worse. Best stay somewhere safe. Have you got some accommodation booked?'

'Yes, everything is sorted. Thanks for all your help,' Liesel said, purchasing a few items of food for dinner and then heading back to her car. Liesel pulled out her cheese sandwich while deciding what to do next. The shopkeeper was right: she should stay somewhere safe.

A beeping sound made her jump. Three texts came through from her boyfriend:

```
Call me, Leez. I've been trying
to phone you for days. Call me!
```

I'm in London. Flight was long.
Boring. Missed you. Freezing cold!

Flying up first thing tmrw.
Meet u at village pub as agreed.
Don't be late.

Can't wait to see you. It's been
way too long.

Hope you haven't changed your
mind! The castle isn't open to
the public, so don't get any ideas
about taking a trip up there.
I know what ur like! Remember,
curiosity killed that damn cat.

Yeah, but satisfaction brought it back!

Liesel turned the phone off. 'Sorry mate, no reception here!' With only one day left to herself, she wanted to enjoy it. Just one day to make the biggest decision of her life! Right now, she didn't have time for guilt or obligation.

Although she'd been in Scotland for barely 48 hours, it was starting to feel like she'd always been here. Tomorrow she'd meet Duncan at the village pub. They'd not seen each other in four long months.

Visiting Europe was her big overseas experience, and Liesel wanted to do it alone. It was important, she told him, that she had this space. Reluctantly, he let her go. Liesel insisted that she couldn't continue their life without some time apart from him. Duncan had argued with her at every turn, but in the end he let her go on the condition they shared a week in the Scottish Highlands.

9

Time was ticking far too quickly for her liking. Liesel needed a get-out clause, but couldn't find one. Or, at least, not one which was honest. The last thing she wanted to do was break his heart. Perhaps, though, she'd feel differently when she saw him again. After all, the past few months had brought so many interesting events and people into her life, that maybe she'd grown enough as a person that she could comfortably settle into her relationship again.

Try as she might, though, Liesel couldn't get Isaac Heathfield out of her head, or the sad story surrounding his home. Never in her life had she been in a castle. It enchanted Liesel that his ancestral home had a longer history of white settlement than her own country.

Instead of heading back to the old fishing hut that she'd hired, she decided to take a drive. Just a short drive, she told herself. What harm could it do to get a glimpse of the castle? It's not like Isaac Heathfield would notice her or anything. The shopkeeper's words of warning were soon cast out of her mind. The storm wasn't *that* bad.

Within minutes she was down Iona Road, marvelling at the views before her. The loch was everything she'd imagined. Duncan was right. It was definitely a place to visit; dark, dismal, and stunningly beautiful in a remote, haunted way.

Liesel ignored the pewter clouds with their angry tones, and turned her back on the wild winds whipping up the water at the loch. The lightning strikes didn't scare her off, either. Not one bit. In fact, lightning enlivened her. Even as a young child, her parents couldn't bring her inside during a thunderstorm. They'd despair when she'd dance barefoot in the rain, lightning zapping like the forked tongue of a snake searching the air.

Liesel discovered that it was just a short drive to the castle. The turrets teased her from above the tree line. *I'll be back in no time*, she told herself. *Then I'll protect myself from the storm*. It was getting darker by the minute, and Liesel knew that she had to hurry up if she wanted to see the place. The Sun went down early at this time of the year, and with the clouds blocking out all light, she began to feel that her castle-glimpsing adventure wasn't going to happen. At least not today, anyway.

By the time she was halfway up the mountain, there were branches strewn all over the road. A full Moon occasionally bared itself when fast-moving clouds tore apart from each other in the driving winds. The night felt eerie, but Liesel told herself that it was just her imagination. The castle wouldn't really be haunted, or else he wouldn't live there. Or would he?

'He'll be glad of the company,' she said out loud, as if trying to convince herself. 'Oh yes, the mysterious Isaac will be grateful for some light-hearted chit-chat on this stormy night.' Laughing at her boldness, Liesel ignored the warning signs Mother Nature was throwing her way.

Driving was getting dangerous. For a moment, she wondered if perhaps the village shopkeeper was right: she should be taking cover somewhere, not seeking a Scottish adventure! Liesel thought she glimpsed some lights in the distance. Maybe it was her imagination. Darkness now cast its veil around the mountainside, but then the flicker of sallow lights lured her closer, closer…and then she couldn't believe her eyes: it *was* the castle. There was no way she could turn back now. Not now that she was almost there. Determination kicked in, and she drove on towards her destination.

'Ready or not, Mr Heathfield, here I come!' she cackled, mimicking the witches of her childhood fairytales. One thing she was sure of was that she was in a playful mood, and what man could resist that? Yes, he'd enjoy her company.

Liesel had no idea what she'd do when she knocked on Isaac Heathfield's front door. Perhaps he'd invite her in for malt whisky by the fire? It sure was bitterly cold. Of course he'd invite her in. Heck, he might even let her stay the night in a spare room. There'd have to be a spare room in a building that size. If he was offended by her turning up uninvited, she could laugh it off as a trait of her Australian roots: brash and bold! The only thing certain in her mind was that she wanted to see this castle for herself. And, with that thought, she slowly drove up the hill; her eyes on the muted lights ahead of her. Excitement tingled in her bones. Of everything she'd done during her four-month tour of Europe, nothing compared to this moment. The thrill of driving in the storm, lightning flashes tempting her towards another existence, the intermittent ghostly glimpses of a pearl-coloured, round-faced Moon, and the lure of wan castle lights made her pulse beat rapidly. No, she shouldn't be sheltering from the storm; she needed to be right in the centre of it.

Isaac Heathfield was feeling twitchy about the storm. Thundersnow was rare, and meant the atmosphere was extremely unstable. Just hours before, he'd sent his staff of five home for the weekend, and hoped they'd all got there safely. Although he kept to himself, he was fond of the small team he had around him, and protective of their well-being. As lightning struck, once again, and more closely this time, he recalled his last conversation just hours before.

'Mr Heathfield, are you sure you want to have the weekend to yourself? You could let the other staff go home, and I could stay on and fetch your meals.'

'Adalene, I'm perfectly capable of looking after myself for a few days. Go on, go home to your family, and enjoy some time off. You're hardly ever away from this place.'

'There are soups and casseroles in the deep freeze. They're all labelled. Potatoes, leeks, onions, beets and carrots in the pantry. Just take bread from the freezer if you run out of loaves. There's plenty of cheese in the fridge. If you need anything, just call me,' she insisted. 'I know why you want us all to go home, but I could stay here and do my jobs and stay out of your way. You wouldn't even know I was here.'

'Adalene, go home.'

Isaac was firm, but his smile betrayed his affection for the elderly lady who'd lived with him for fifteen years. Adalene was the closest thing to a mother he had, and although their relationship was strictly professional, he was fond of her.

Solitude. That's what he craved. The castle had felt a bit cramped for Isaac's liking, and he just needed some space. A bit of time alone would help him to get his thoughts in order. After he poured some whisky, Isaac silently toasted the air. It was a nod to grief, regret, relief and the solace of therapeutic isolation; and he wondered what the future would bring. *Would life always be like this?* This weekend was the tenth anniversary of his late wife's death, and he didn't want anyone reminding him. Isaac could do that all on his own. Ten years of regret haunted him on a daily basis.

Space. That was what he needed: time and space.

'God, Marylynn, why did you have to do that to me?' he yelled out loud, kicking the wall. 'Why did you have to ruin my life?' Isaac felt every bit as angry with her now as when she died. Everything about that time was wrong.

Even though he tried to control his thoughts, they turned to the weeks after her death: day after day being questioned by police. Investigators turned his home upside down looking for evidence of foul play. When they finally released him, he thought it would be impossible to continue living at Stoneyhill.

The gossip would last the rest of his days. But a nagging voice kept insisting he'd be letting down a long line of men who'd fought to keep this home in the family. It was the voice of duty, of responsibility, of ancestry. So often he wanted to walk away and just start his life over, anonymously, but the voice kept getting louder until he lost sense of what he wanted for himself.

Over the years, the still waters of the loch absorbed some of his pain and all the memories which kept him tied here. It swallowed the angst: a reservoir of confusion, fear, guilt, anger and torment. There were so many times he hated that damn loch, and yet he loved it in equal measure. No wonder the locals called it haunted. If ever there was a troubled piece of water, this was it. Secrets lurked below the surface.

Apart from his staff, there was no one significant in his life. No one to witness his journey. No one to give a damn about him. Isaac Heathfield's life was a solitary one, and he'd designed it to be that way. There was no room for hurt or the complexities of human relationships.

As he moved nearer to the window, he was startled by headlights shining towards his home. 'Who the hell is that?' he yelled, wondering just who had the audacity to come to his castle without an invitation. It was unheard of.

Lightning struck, and he jumped out of his skin. Damn it! Thunder rumbled almost immediately afterwards. For a moment, he felt himself disoriented, as if he'd lost his footing. It was almost as if, though he knew better, he'd been struck by the lightning. A powerful force zapped him. *Don't be stupid,* he muttered.

An imposing figure, Isaac always had to duck when walking through doorways. The regular hikes he enjoyed in the Highlands leant him his taut and toned muscles. Suddenly his body didn't feel strong and powerful. It felt as if it was afflicted by something well out of his control. The storm was close, and it was like the castle itself had been struck, such was the powerful voltage zapping his body.

Isaac stood by the window for some time, running his hand through his dark, slightly curly hair, wondering why the lights weren't getting any closer. Was someone spying on him?

Finally, he'd had enough. Furiously forcing himself into a coat, he braced himself against the howling storm. Or, he wondered, were those torturous sounds actually Marylynn howling? Isaac couldn't be sure. The winds whipped against his skin, raindrops diving into him like darts.

Once he was in the Landrover, he slammed his foot down on the accelerator pedal, and forced his way down the driveway to face the intruder. In the dark of night, he drove closer to the uninvited vehicle. In no time at all, he'd get rid of them. He was close now, perhaps fifty metres from the intruder. Infuriated that his privacy was being violated, he swore out loud.

Isaac was startled to see that the huge, three-hundred-year-old oak tree an ancestor had planted cut the Volkswagen Beetle almost in half. Instinctively, he raced around to see if the people inside were alive. With a pounding heart he assessed the situation. The uninvited visitors had been stopped short by the storm. More than likely they were dead. It wasn't a thought he wanted to entertain.

Isaac shone the torch all around the car.

Just a driver. No passengers.

'Hello!' he yelled. 'Are you okay? Can you hear me?' Howling winds battered him and driving rain pierced his cheeks with sharp pellets. With limited visibility, Isaac felt himself panic. If there was anything he hated, it was being out of control. The shaking of his hands betrayed his strong character. Isaac's life was based on structure and routine, not chaos and confusion.

The driver was unconscious, and bleeding. With adrenaline-fuelled strength, he extricated her from behind the wheel and carried her to his Landrover. It broke every first-aid rule to move her, but there was no way he could leave her here, in the dark, to bleed to death. There was no telling how much blood she'd lost. Isaac surveyed the road through torchlight. The storm was brutal. It was impossible to drive beyond the other side of the tree. Tomorrow he'd have to call for help. But first, he had to get her home. Inside, away from the nasty weather, he'd be able to assess the damage.

Avoiding every pothole in the road, he drove home carefully, and then carried the unresponsive body up two flights of stairs, and placed her on his bed. Who was this girl? What the hell was she doing driving up to the castle? It's not like she could have been lost, not when there were no less than five signs saying: PRIVATE PROPERTY. NO ENTRY.

What sort of person would deliberately ignore such signs? The audacity to ignore a simple instruction! Isaac was furious. When she regained consciousness, he'd give her a piece of his mind. He couldn't abide trespassers. The young woman couldn't have been from around here; the locals knew better than to venture onto Stoneyhill property.

Isaac cursed. He was no nurse! And he certainly didn't want to play caretaker to the law-defying woman who was in his bed! After fumbling through the first-aid gear, he pulled out some cotton wool and disinfectant, muttering and cursing some more. He'd tend to her wounds, and as soon as she regained consciousness then he'd send her on her way.

With everything he needed assembled on the bedside dresser, Isaac began his nursing duties.

Slowly, *tenderly*—in a way which surprised him—he cleaned the wounds, and checked her over for broken bones. The clothes she wore were soaking wet from being carried from one vehicle to another in the storm. Isaac was in two minds about whether it was ethical to undress an unconscious girl. Or was she a woman? Sure, she had the body of a woman, but her face had an innocent youthfulness about it. Isaac convinced himself that seeing her naked was better than her getting a chill. The weather was cold enough as it was, without her being soaked to the bone. This was the last thing he needed.

Of all the times to send his maid home! He'd have to wash and dry these damn clothes himself. The repetitive tick of the clock made him acutely aware that he was no longer alone. *So much for having the weekend to mull through old memories without anyone invading his privacy.* Damn it!

Isaac paced the room. This was not how he wanted to spend the weekend. The only thing Isaac Heathfield wanted was to be alone, without anyone disturbing his thoughts. And this woman was disturbing his thoughts! The last time a woman had done that was when he watched Marylynn throw her body down the main staircase of Stoneyhill, tumbling down like a ragdoll until, at last, she lay on the floor below. Still, so very still. When it happened, he raced down the stairs to tell her things would be alright. That they'd find a way to work through their problems, but all he found was a body without a pulse. For half an hour he'd tried to bring life back to the corpse. The paramedics pronounced her dead at the scene. Isaac couldn't think straight. How could life change so quickly? His thoughts returned to the woman in his bed.

Who was she? And why the hell didn't she turn back at the very first sign? Five signs, at various points on the two-mile-long drive to the castle through ancient woodland, were large, and written in bold: impossible to miss. And she, this creature in his bed, ignored *all* of them.

Isaac covered her bare body with a sheet and several woollen blankets. Not a girl, he said to himself. *A woman.* Lightning struck, and then he realised it was a shock which ran through his body, and had nothing to do with the storm outside. How could someone who wasn't even awake have this much impact on him and render him senseless? He reminded himself that he'd only had one glass of whisky. What was he thinking? Of course she didn't have any effect on him.

Isaac built up the fire in the old grate, and when it felt cosy and warm in the room, he walked down the hallway and then phoned the hospital.

'I'm sorry, Mr Heathfield, we can't send an ambulance up. The roads are closed over there. Dozens of trees have come down. They'll need to be removed before traffic can flow again. It's not safe for anyone to be travelling tonight. Keep the patient warm, and don't leave her alone under any circumstance.'

Isaac hung up the phone. 'Closed roads?' he yelled across the hallway. What century were they living in? Keep the patient warm? This was not how the weekend was meant to be! Damn it. Damn her!

Isaac walked the length of the hallway in the left wing of the castle at least a dozen times. Every part of his brain was searching for answers to this dilemma. He had to get rid of her, and fast. She was not part of his plans.

Eventually he came back into the bedroom, and pulled up a chair next to her. To his surprise, he found himself gently touching the top of her head, his hands smoothing down her dark hair. As she lay there, she looked so helpless, and it jolted him to realise that she actually needed him. This stranger needed him to protect her. Anger gave way to something wholly unfamiliar.

Before long, he nicknamed her Lightning. Isaac told himself that she deserved a name, at least. And until he found out who she was, he'd just call her that. Little did he know, that was her childhood nickname born from her love of dancing outdoors during thunder storms.

At just after midnight, Isaac crawled into bed beside her. Without doubt, he could have slept in any one of a number of rooms. Heck, he could have even slept in the armchair. It would have been the gentlemanly thing to do but, he reasoned, she needed him as close as possible. If she woke up, she'd be scared, and he convinced himself that he could reassure her immediately if he was right next to her.

'Don't leave the patient alone,' was the instruction he'd received. Isaac listened to her soft breathing, and studied the way her lips curved up into a rosebud shape. They were deep red, and her eyelashes were dark, just like her shoulder-length, wavy hair.

An unconscious woman in his bed. Just what he needed! Isaac was about to roll over and turn his back to her, when he became aware, frustratingly aware, that he found her deeply attractive and he instinctively lifted his finger to touch her cheek. So soft and smooth. Isaac surveyed her in great detail. An exquisite painting, her features were classical: high cheekbones; pert, sculpted nose; flawless, olive-tanned skin, perfect ears with lobes that begged him to lean over and kiss them. There was something so strikingly beautiful about her, that it wouldn't have surprised him if she'd just stepped out of a 1920s black and white movie.

'What are you doing here?' he muttered beneath his breath. 'Why here? Why me?'

Oh my, she was beautiful. There was something about her that reminded him of a deer gracefully grazing in the woodland. Fragile, beautiful, otherworldly. She smelt of the loch, and of Winter rain. Abruptly, he moved to the far side of the bed.

With pounding heart, he turned his back on her. The sooner he got this woman out of his bed and down to a hospital, the better. The last thing he needed in his life was a woman; especially one as beautiful her.

On sentry duty, Isaac watched over her by the flicker of candlelight, monitoring her breathing, checking her pulse, and from time to time touching her cheek. Those stolen moments called to him; beseeching him to open his heart. Isaac couldn't explain why he felt the need to hold her hand from time to time. If he didn't know better, he'd have thought the soft murmurings he heard throughout the night were from his late grandmother: *don't be afraid, boy.*

Dawn came slowly, as it often did on these crisp January mornings. Isaac stoked the fire, and brought another basket of wood up from downstairs. There was no sign of change in the young woman.

'Don't worry, Lightning, we'll get you better. You'll be home in no time.'

A pang of something, of which he knew not, crashed hard into his chest. How ridiculous. Of course she'd be home soon. She had no place here. What *was* that stupid thought trying to ease its way into the corner of his mind?

Despite the nurse telling him not to leave her alone, Isaac headed to the kitchen and made a strong brew of coffee. After the night he had, he sure needed it! Isaac had been taunted all night long by the beautiful woman within arms' reach. For a while, he looked out the window, down the driveway, at her car.

Ignoring the nurse's instructions, Isaac abandoned his coffee and drove the Landrover down the driveway for a better look. Perhaps there were answers there to her identity, and more importantly, what the hell she was doing coming to his castle in the dark of night. The storm damage was extensive. Trees down everywhere.

21

The car was battered, and a write-off. An electrical shock tore right through him. Again. It was a miracle that she wasn't dead. Had she been coming to visit him? Why? He'd never seen her in his life. Who was she?

Isaac found himself feeling grateful that she was in his bed, and not dead.

For some time, he thoroughly searched the car for signs of her identity. There was a handbag, and a violin case. Even though he tried several times, he couldn't get under the bonnet, as it was too badly damaged and under the guard of a weighty, splintered tree trunk. *No change of clothes for you then, Lightning*, he muttered. Isaac surveyed the scene. How did he get her out of there alive? It seemed impossible.

When he entered his bedroom, he saw that she was still unconscious. It went against everything he believed in: he hated the thought of looking inside a woman's handbag—it was wrong—but he assured himself that it was the right thing to do. There was probably a husband or boyfriend, or parents who'd be worried about her.

Isaac emptied the contents onto the end of the bed. Navy-blue passport with a kangaroo and an emu emblazoned on the front, in gold; flight tickets; wild-rose deodorant; lime lip balm; mirror; sewing kit; mobile phone; a purse with two hundred pounds; driver's licence; Medicare card; a small book on 19th century European violinists; postcards of the village; a dozen postcards from across Europe; plastic wrap of a cheese sandwich.

'Liesel Eather. Australian?' he said out loud, looking at her passport. 'So far from home, Lightning. What are you doing here?' The stamps inside indicated she'd been to Dublin, Florence, Hungary, Berlin, Paris and Belgium in recent months. Isaac searched for contact details; names of anyone he could get in touch with. The mobile phone was locked. He tried using the birth date in her passport as the pin number. That didn't work. It was her birthday in a few weeks and he hoped she'd be awake to celebrate it.

So, she was a 26-year-old Australian on her way up the mountain to see him. And she played violin. That's all he had. Perhaps she'd been staying locally, and had an address book or something there.

At some point, if she didn't wake up, he'd go to the pub and ask questions. Surely someone must have seen her before she travelled to the castle?

Isaac stayed by her side all morning, touching her forehead from time to time. 'Don't worry, Lightning, we'll soon have you fixed up and on your way,' he whispered, and felt a jolt inside, as if he was once again given electric shock treatment. Then he quickly threw the idea out of his head. *Of course she had to go!* Why would he even consider that she might stay here?

The Hermit and the Musician

It was late afternoon when Isaac was distracted by an unfamiliar sound. A small moan escaped Liesel's lips. When he looked up from his book, he noticed that she was trying to talk.

'Shhh. You're safe, Lightning,' he said softly. 'You've been in an accident, but you're okay now.' He edged closer to her, and sat on the side of her bed.

Isaac was out of his comfort zone. He wasn't a nurturer. No, Isaac Heathfield was a hermit, who preferred his own company, and liked nothing better than being in a room on his own. If he had a choice, he didn't want people around him. Relationships of any description were fraught with trouble. So why the hell was he sitting here playing nursemaid? Everything about this situation was wrong.

It was counter-intuitive to the life he knew, but he reached out his hand to reassure her; to offer her a lifeline and help her feel secure. Liesel's skin was soft beneath his, and he felt his hand tingling the second he held hers.

'Where am I?' she mumbled.

'The Scottish Highlands. Does that mean anything to you?' he asked gently.

'Who are you?' she asked, closing her eyes again.

'Isaac. You're safe here, Liesel.'

'Liesel? Oh my head!' she moaned as she gripped her forehead to stifle the shooting pains. 'Who is Liesel?'

'Liesel Eather. I'm sorry, I was looking for your identity. Your passport says you're Liesel Eather, from Australia.'

'Australia? My name is Liesel?' She asked, opening and closing her eyes, her lashes fluttering.

'Who did you say I was? Where am I?' Her eyes opened and closed again. 'Who is Liesel?'

Oh God. Isaac hung his head in exasperation. Not only did he have a strange, albeit beautiful, woman in his bed, she didn't know who she was! What the hell was he going to do with her? Though he knew what he wanted to do with that beautiful body, he immediately threw such a reckless and incendiary desire out of the window. It was totally inappropriate.

'I'll be back in a minute,' he whispered, and went into the hallway to speak to the nurse at the hospital.

'Memory loss is quite common in situations like this, Mr Heathfield. I appreciate your concern, but it's probably short term. Just keep looking after her.'

'Is that it? Is that the best advice you can give me? This woman is a stranger and she needs more than my nursing incompetence.'

'Given the situation, sir, neither of you has much choice in the matter. We're at the end of the phone if there's anything else you need to know.'

What a nightmare! Chained to the bedside of a woman who doesn't even know her name, and no way of driving her down to the local infirmary; he was stuck. Stuck! A voice inside his head mocked him and said: *Struck*. You've been struck!

By lightning? He silently replied to the voice.

Yes, Lightning, the voice laughed.

'Do you know why you were driving to see me?' Isaac asked her, trying to make sense of why she was travelling to the castle on a stormy night.

'Driving?' she asked, then tried sitting up in bed. 'Oh my head!' She groaned, and slid back beneath the covers.

'Yes, you were driving to see me. You drove through a violent storm. Why were you coming here?'

'I don't know. Who did you say I was?'

'Liesel. Liesel Eather. You're from Australia.'

'Oh.'

Isaac watched her drift in and out of sleep for a few hours, then he came back to her bedside. 'There's a toilet through that door if you need one, and a small washbasin.'

'Okay,' she said, smiling up at him.

Isaac left the room, and came back ten minutes later to check on her. Although he knew he shouldn't leave her side, he found it too distracting watching her the whole time.

'Are you hungry?' he asked.

'Yes, I think I am. I'm feeling a bit better.'

'I'll be back shortly. Don't get out of bed.' Isaac put another blanket on her. It was chilly, and the last thing she needed was to get a cold. It was the last thing *he* needed. If she caught a cold, he'd hardly be able to turn her out into the elements.

A little while later, Isaac returned with a pottery bowl of steaming leek and potato soup, and soda-bread croutons, grateful that Adalene, his maid of fifteen years, had left several portions of various meals in the freezer. He'd also made Liesel an espresso.

'This is tasty,' Liesel said. 'You're a really good cook!'

Isaac turned away so she couldn't read his face. Well, he was hardly going to admit that he rarely cooked. There was no need when he was surrounded by capable staff. This wasn't the time to say that anything mundane was always performed by someone else so he could concentrate on the bigger things of life.

'Since neither of us knows much about who I am, perhaps you can tell me about yourself, Isaac. If I'm going to be stuck here, then I may as well get to know who my rescuer is. And, by the way, where are my clothes? I'm completely naked beneath these blankets. I don't imagine I was driving like this.' And as she smiled, he felt one of his defences go down.

Isaac found that she was even more beautiful—if that was actually possible—now that she was awake. As her smile melted his heart, he told himself: get a grip.

'They're drying. You were soaked. I...I had to get you out of them. And if you had any suitcases in the bonnet of your Volkswagen, I wasn't able to get them due to a rather large tree getting in the way. I promise I didn't look,' he smiled.

When her spontaneous laughter filled the room, it made lightning strike his body again. Who was she? How did she have this affect on him?

'I'll just have to take your word for it!' Once again, her bright laughter put him at ease, and he felt himself relaxing for the first time since that fateful moment when he found her in the car, unsure whether she was dead or alive. Just remembering her there: stuck behind the wheel, blood dripping down her face, lifeless: his heart skipped several beats.

This was wholly unexpected: he was rapidly falling for her. The way she laughed, and her broad smile, enchanted him. Isaac was smitten but he had to get rid of her. She was dangerous! This girl could undo everything he'd spent the past ten years building up, including his defences! Isaac searched his mind for something to distract the warmth that was building up. As nice as the feeling was, he knew it couldn't last; wouldn't last. It was time to hasten her recovery.

'So, who are you, Isaac?' and she said it in such a way that it would have been rude not to answer her.

'There's not much to tell you. I was born here in this place, and I'll probably die here.'

'That's it? My rescuer sums up who he is by where he was born and where he'll die? What about all the years in between? Don't they have any meaning?'

Isaac wanted to tell her the truth: that life is what you make it, and the only meaning in his life came from his work.

'I live here for most of the year, but travel away quite often. I enjoy walking through heather-covered glens, and down by the loch. My ancestral heritage is strong, and is what keeps me living here. I prefer my own company, and keep to myself most of the time. I don't actually like people. That's who I am, Liesel. That's the truth. I'm a loner, and I like it that way.'

How much should he tell her, he wondered. Isaac was a private person, and really didn't feel comfortable sharing his deepest darkest secrets with a perfect stranger. And she *was* perfect, or so his wayward thoughts kept telling him as he wrestled them to the ground.

'Interesting,' she said, locking her eyes with his.

'*Interesting?*' What the hell did she mean by that? There was nothing interesting about this situation. Annoying, that's what it was. But not interesting!

'Yes, interesting,' she replied confidently. Far too confidently for his liking. 'You like being on your own, and now you're stuck in a room with a stranger. Interesting.' It was the funniest thing she'd ever heard, or at least it *would* have been if she could remember anything!

Isaac couldn't help but laugh with her. Perhaps she was right. The situation did have an edge of comedy to it.

'Ironic, huh?' he said.

'I'm sorry,' she replied softly, trying to express her empathy for his dilemma.

'What for?' he asked, perplexed by her apology.

'Gatecrashing your party-for-one.'

'I don't think you had much choice! Though I would like to know why you ignored *five* signs telling you that you were on private property and that made it quite clear you had no permission to continue driving along the road.'

'Sounds like I was pretty determined to see you, doesn't it?' Liesel looked him up and down, taking in his lean-but-firm body. A small moan of pleasure echoed beneath her chest. Isaac told himself it was his imagination. Of course she didn't think he was attractive! Ridiculous. The woman was virtually an invalid. What sort of woman would blatantly express her desire like that? Certainly no woman he'd ever met before.

The conversation continued casually for some time, but more than once Isaac wondered if she was flirting with him. How was that even possible? His job, his *only* job, was to nurse her back to recovery so she could leave and get back to her life.

Isaac was conflicted. Although he was quickly growing to like Liesel, he knew that their easy companionship couldn't last; wouldn't last. They both had lives to get on with. An internal tug of war raged: he wanted her, and he didn't want her!

More than once he had to remind himself that the only thing he wanted was to be alone this weekend:

time to reflect on the anniversary of his late wife's untimely death, and everything that had happened in the years between. There was not a chance in the world of that happening while Miss Sunshine was sitting an arm's distance away laughing and smiling.

'Would you like a bath or a shower?' Isaac asked, trying to think of something else besides her naked body beneath the blankets, but the question only made things worse. It occurred to him that he hoped she couldn't tell how aroused he was, or the impact her slight moan had had on him.

'If it's not too much trouble, then yes please. Do you have a dressing gown I could borrow?'

'Of course. I'll run a bath, and sort you some towels. Stay under those blankets!' Even though he tried to be stern, Isaac found himself responding with a slight smile. He liked her. He *really* liked her. This was not good. Not good at all! How on Earth did that happen so quickly? Isaac hadn't even gotten around to giving her a piece of his mind about trespassing. Somehow they'd just glided over that misdemeanour.

Never mind, as soon as she was standing again he'd send her on her merry little Australian way. And then she could take her smile somewhere else; to someone else's party!

Contradictions coursed through his entire body, and rendered him so frustrated and happy at the same time that he had moments of forgetting how damn cross he was that she'd violated the trespass notices to Stoneyhill.

Isaac hummed an old Gaelic tune as he entered the bathroom. It made himself chuckle.

'When was the last time you sang or hummed anything?' he said out loud. 'You're a miserable git.

30

Don't go ruining your reputation by singing a tune or dancing a jig!'

A large bath, perched on huge iron claws, sat in the centre of the expansive bathroom. The walls were built from Scottish stone, and the height of the ceiling leant over the room in quite an imposing way. Isaac filled the tub with steaming water, and gathered some items together that Liesel might find of use, including heather and wildflower-honey soap, a book to read, and a face cloth. Isaac had missed the touch a woman could bring to the home: delicate scents, beautiful flowers, and a song from her lips. Don't even think about it, he told himself when the fragments of nostalgia permeated the room alongside the steam.

When he returned, a few minutes later, he passed Liesel a gown, and said 'Here, let me help you.'

Isaac noticed that she blushed a little, and reminded her that she needed all the help she could get. Liesel was wobbly on her feet, and held his arm as they left the bedroom to go to the bathroom across the hallway.

'I don't suppose I make a habit of being naked in front of men I don't know, but then, I don't know anything about who I am. Maybe I do this all the time!'

The lightness in her laugh assured Isaac that she was taking the situation in her stride. He wasn't entirely sure he could get used to that accent though. It was so far removed from the refined way he spoke his vowels, and the diction drummed into him during thirteen years of a military-style English boarding school. The way Liesel spoke, it was as if every day was a holiday; her tones relaxed and joy-filled; and he loved the warmth that each word exuded. Maybe she would grow on him after all?

How could Lightning be so relaxed, he wondered, when she was in a strange country and didn't even know who she was?

The bathroom was steamy. True to his word, he'd arranged some towels. They were large and fluffy, made from fine Egyptian cotton. Nearby was a glass of chilled apple juice. A candelabra held six flickering beeswax candles; and a CD playing Baroque music filled the room with calming sounds.

The relaxed ambience of the bathroom made her swoon.

'I almost feel like a princess. If I could twirl around in glee I would. This room is beautiful. Magical.'

In that moment, Isaac wanted to tell her that she looked like a princess, but started to back out of the bathroom. Isaac was determined to keep his thoughts to himself. It was important not to encourage her in any way. The only role he had in her life was to help her become well enough to continue her travels. Nothing more, nothing less. There were times in life when imagination served you well, but this was not one of them.

'Call me if you need anything. I'll wait in the hallway,' he said, and then left her alone. After a few minutes, she called him back.

'Can you stay in here with me?' she asked, her tone making it clear that she hoped he wouldn't refuse.

'Don't you want some privacy?' he replied, his head peering around the doorway₁

'No, I want some...Right now, I need to feel safe. You're the only thing familiar to me in a world of unknowns. I'd prefer it if I didn't lose sight of you.'

Touched by her vulnerability, he said 'Of course. I won't go anywhere.'

Isaac helped her out of his dressing gown, and hung it on the back of a chair. As she stepped into the warm water, he tried not to look at the gentle curves of her tanned body. Every inch of her had a vibrant, healthy, golden glow, with no sign of any areas not being exposed to sunlight. Isaac caught himself wondering if she sunbathed naked, and a soft groan left his being.

'Are you okay?' she asked, concerned at how he'd abruptly moved away from her.

'Yes. I'm fine.'

'This room is huge. Who has a bathroom like this? It's bigger than a house. This is what you'd expect in a castle!'

'This *is* a castle, Liesel. Stoneyhill Castle. It's my ancestral home.'

'Castle? No wonder I feel like a princess! But aren't castles supposed to have butlers, maids and men in fine suits? You don't look like you own a castle,' she giggled softly, taking in the sight of him dressed in faded denim jeans and a thick, hand-knitted, cream-coloured woollen jumper.

'And what exactly does a castle owner look like?' he laughed. 'Anyway, I sent my staff home for the weekend!'

'Oh.'

'Yes. There's Adalene, my maid of fifteen years. Maximus is my butler. Jerome, Sebastian and Ryder are general help.'

A few minutes later she looked up at him and said, 'A castle? We're alone here? In a castle?'

'Yes, we're alone. Just you and me in a ridiculously large castle in the middle of nowhere.'

'Sounds fun!' she smiled, mischievously splashing the water with her hands so a bit would spray up on

Isaac's face; he didn't entirely see the funny side of her playful antics.

Fun? *Fun!* Isaac Heathfield didn't do fun! For God's sake, he was a dour Scotsman even if he did sound like an Englishman! Lightning needed to go. This woman needed to leave his 'fun' castle as quickly as she'd arrived. No, there was absolutely no room in his neatly ordered life for something as frivolous as fun! He felt his head was spinning. Isaac wondered what thoughts were going through her mind, and if they were nearly as dangerous as the fantasies he was entertaining. How on Earth did he get into this situation?

Nothing in his thirty-five years of life had prepared him for this moment. Nothing at all. Nothing in his expensive education taught him how to handle gypsy-like women who had free spirits. Actually, it didn't teach him anything about women at all, and perhaps that had been the problem all along.

They sat in silence for a while, listening to the music, then Isaac asked 'Would you like me to wash your back or your hair?'

Their eyes caught. Lightning struck both of them.

'Did you feel that?' she asked. 'The electricity was shocking,' she said as she grabbed hold of the side of the tub. 'Isaac, did you *feel* that?'

Isaac wasn't entirely sure that he liked this electrical surge sneaking up on him, sending shock waves through his body, and forcing him to be incapable of clear thinking. Everything about him, about his life, was controlled, structured, solid: secure. Everything about being with her was wild, crazy, out of control: shaky foundations. If he was certain of anything, it was that being with her made everything uncertain: unpredictable. Isaac had never been so terrified in his life. The sooner she was out of here, the quicker he could regain his strong sense of self. And he *was* a strong man. Life had made him that way.

'Yes, please. I'd love you to wash my hair.'

And there it was, that smile, once again dissolving his resolves.

Isaac filled the large pitcher with warm water, and let it run down her hair and tanned back. With each rush of warmth down her skin, Liesel sighed, unable to contain the pleasure. With gentle movements, he massaged the shampoo into a rich lather. Even though he washed his own hair every morning, washing *her* hair was the most erotic thing he'd done in his life. Isaac was beginning to wonder if he'd even been alive before now.

As he sat behind her, on a low chair, his fingers and thumbs gently pressing into her scalp, in slow circular movements, his eyes took in the view before him: abundant breasts, curvaceous hips, a triangle of dark hair tantalising the path to rich delights, long legs stretching the distance of the huge claw-foot bathtub. A small groan escaped from under his tortured breath.

'Would you like me to finish it?' she asked, realising that her pleasure was his pain.

'No, I'll finish what I started.' Isaac's breath was ragged.

If Lightning was going to stay here as his guest, he needed to get a grip of his emotions and get himself back under control. Right now, he felt as if he was in the eye of the storm, being battered by hurricane-force winds over which he was powerless.

It's just lust, he told himself.

You've been on your own for too long. It's only natural to feel temptation. You're a man for goodness sake!

Liesel found herself wanting to turn around and to meet him half way. But was it right to kiss a complete stranger? She didn't even know who *she* was! The chemistry was explosive. A raw force pierced the air between them.

Isaac rinsed her thick, lustrous hair, and conditioned it, continuing with the gentle massage. It lulled them both into a state of deep relaxation.

'Would you wash my back, too' she asked, her breath staccato-heavy, not wanting him to stop touching her; desperate for their connection to stay intact. The room around them appeared to flash with a luminous glow, stirring up enough atmospheric turbulence to wake the dead.

Isaac moaned. If he could get into that bathtub with her right now, he would. Instead, he slowly soaped her back, and then rinsed the suds away. And afterwards, he left his hand there, against the small of her back, for a few seconds. So desperate to put his arms around her, and hold Liesel close, he almost forgot who he was, and where they were, and how they were in this position. They were complete strangers to each other. A cracking sound clapped through the air. Or was the explosion internal?

Who was she? Why did he feel so drawn in her direction? It was as if he had no say over the gravitational pull which threatened to destroy everything he knew.

Later, he held her hand and helped her to stand up. Liesel stepped out of the tub into his waiting arms as he wrapped a luxurious bath towel around her. They stood, looking into each other's eyes for the longest time, as if reading each other. Her eyes were chocolate brown, and shone like headlights in the dark night; and his were deep green, like the loch, full of depth and darkness and hinted of unknown dangers. *Lightning!* In those moments, it was as if they read back through time, and glimpsed into the future. It was a place beyond words, too beautiful for logic. And fragile. Terribly fragile. Perhaps that's what scared him the most. The foundations of whatever it was that caused the cacophonous boom and rapturous flash between them was based on nothing but lust: a primal force as old as man. At least that's what he told himself: He was a normal, healthy, red-blooded male. His reactions to her were to be *expected*. Isaac told himself that he wouldn't be a man if he didn't have some bodily response to her. Isaac willed himself not to read anything into it. That would only be asking for trouble.

How the hell was he going to get through the night? It would be the longest night of his life.

Isaac dried her, from the top of her head to the tips of her toes, and everywhere in between. Slow, careful, deliberate drying; he was tender with every touch. Their eyes never left each other. In some strange way, he felt as if he had just made love to her; he was so overwhelmed by the feeling of patting her dry with the soft towel, and breathing her into his being. Liesel was mesmerising.

Like a wild stallion's hooves ripping up the dry earth beneath him, his heart pounded beneath his ribs. Liesel's eyes followed his every movement telling him to come closer, to stay close, and to be close. She was a gravitational whirlpool—*quicksand*—luring him with the irresistible nectar of seductive femininity. No wonder he felt so powerless; he was being taken hostage in his own home. And all she was guilty of was looking at him! But oh how she looked at him.

'You know me better than I know myself,' she whispered, as he carried her naked body back to bed. It was a chivalrous act, picking her up like that. Isaac wasn't sure what possessed him, other than the deep desire to want to look after her no matter the price to his well-organised existence. And he was clear about one thing: she was costing him dearly.

'I don't know if that's a blessing or a curse,' he groaned, covering her with the blankets. 'Stay warm. I'll stoke the fire up again.'

'No need for that. Isaac, come to bed. Come and keep me warm. Please.'

'No Liesel. I can't do that. It's not fair to you. I'd be taking advantage of you when you're at your most vulnerable. It's not right. I'm a gentleman, not a...'

'Don't you want to make love with me?' she asked.

Isaac tried not to laugh at the impromptu frown between her eyebrows and perplexed expression.

'More than I've ever wanted anything in my whole life.' Did those words just come out of his mouth? Where was his control? What was he thinking! Isaac's thoughts turned back to when they stood in the bathroom, and he dried every inch of her body with the towel. Not once did she grimace or flinch. Liesel had looked at him for every long second, and as she did so he felt his body pounding with the needs of an untamed man.

'So, what's stopping you?' she asked. 'Why won't you make love with me?'

'Stopping me? There is nothing about this situation that's simple or straightforward. I'm afraid that if I allowed myself that delicacy, I'd not be able to face you walking away from here.' The realisation of what she meant to him hurtled through his veins like an explosive. How was this even possible? Relationships were planned, arranged by others, even; they didn't come to you on the winds of a storm! Or did they?

Isaac summoned up all his willpower and walked out of the bedroom. 'Ring the bell if there's anything you need,' he called as he turned into the hallway. A cold shower. That's what he needed. No, that wouldn't be enough. A freezer. Isaac needed a freezer.

Within two steps, the bell was ringing.

'What's wrong?' he asked, alarmed at her immediate call for him. Isaac stood at the doorway, as if it offered protection from the seductress before his eyes.

'I need you, Isaac.' Liesel sat up in bed, the blankets falling off her shoulders to reveal her bare breasts.

Isaac's eyes lowered and took in the sight of her: those dark nipples taunting him, teasing him, luring him. There was no way he was going to go anywhere near her. Not now, not ever!

A low-octave groan grumbled in the base of his body. Two forces fought furiously within him: *stay or go?*

'What you need, young lady,' he said firmly, mustering his strength, 'is to get back your wellbeing so we can get you out on the road. You don't need me.'

Isaac walked back into the room, blood pulsing through his veins, and sat on the side of the bed, holding her hand. Even as he did so, he knew it was a bad move. The closer he got to her, the less chance there was of remaining in control.

A phosphorescent turbulence roared through his flesh and he fought with every inch of his being to resist her.

'I can't do this, Liesel. I can't allow myself the luxury of falling in...of falling for you; and I'm afraid that's what would happen. Everything about you makes me lose my senses.'

'But why? Why do you have to hold back? Surely you feel the same as I do? It's palpable. I can almost feel the electricity in the air. It's frightening, yes, but it's also the most powerful thing I've ever felt in my life. We shouldn't deny this.'

'You don't even remember your life!' he said, closing his eyes in frustration. Isaac wanted to feel angry at her logic, but he couldn't. She was actually right. He stalled for time. 'You could be married for all I know, or have a boyfriend, or children. I know nothing about you.' Once again, Isaac turned to walk away, his fists clenched in aggravation. Of course he wanted her! The truth was that he wanted her in every way possible, and he'd never known such fear. It defied who he was, and everything he'd done in his life.

'Do you want to know about me, Isaac?'

'Of course I do!'

'Come to bed with me then. Put your arms around me, and hold me. Just hold me. Nothing else.'

Now his resistance was down. Damn it! Isaac Heathfield was a man of control. Conservative. Strong. Reliable. There was no room in his life for spontaneity. Heathfield men never did anything without giving it intense thought and planning. There was no way on God's green Earth that he was going to make love with her.

With each deep breath, he slowly regained his fortitude. Liesel might well have been a dream come true, but Isaac chastened himself: *there's no room in your life for dreams*.

Like a skilled seductress, she smiled at him, and pulled the bedclothes back even further as if to say 'what are you waiting for?' Making space in the bed for him, she patted the sheet beside her. 'Come on.' Goosebumps pricked her skin. The air was bitterly cold, but all Isaac felt was a roaring heat.

'I can't...' he said.

'Can't or won't?' Her face was warm and inviting, and he couldn't believe that he was actually standing next to the most beautiful woman he'd ever seen and was rejecting her advances. What was wrong with him? *Are you insane*? a voice inside his head asked. That was the trouble. There were just too many damned voices in his head. Some telling him to stay away from the storm; others saying: *rush headlong into it. Let Lightning consume you.*

'Isaac, didn't anyone ever teach you that what you miss out on today, you can't catch up on tomorrow?'

'When did you get so wise?' And he couldn't help laughing. 'For a girl,' he corrected himself, 'for a *woman* who doesn't remember anything, you're pretty smart.'

'I'll wait for you for as long as you need,' she whispered. 'I know you want to make love with me. I can see it in your eyes. Why are you fighting it?'

Isaac watched her shivering from the cold. There was only one way to warm her up. His body was like a raging inferno. Clothes, torn off, were discarded like yesterday's newspaper. And then he lay beside her: both of them naked. There were no secrets now. His body would show her exactly what he was feeling. He'd do anything to have her, but not like this. This was wrong! Stalling for time, side-tracking her with conversation, or a simple backrub, these would help her feel safe, and loved. He understood that. What harm would a simple hug do? It would help her to feel secure, and surely that would help her recovery?

Liesel reached over for him, and touched his firm chest; her fingers tracing his twirls of dark, curly hair. With each movement, she felt his breathing become shallow and rapid.

'What are you scared of, Isaac?' she asked, breathing in the scent of his body which smelled faintly of Scots pine and milky coffee.

'You.'

Liesel could feel him discarding his fears under her soft touches. How was it possible for one human to have this effect on another? Butter melting in the sunlight, that's how it felt when her hands soothed his skin. Everything solid in his life was rapidly disappearing.

'Why?' She tried to read his eyes, searching the deep waters of his facial loch, wanting answers; desperate to uncover the source of his pain. 'I won't hurt you. I promise.'

'I know nothing about you, Liesel, but of this I'm sure: I don't believe you would go to bed with a strange man. Not for one minute.'

'You're no stranger to me, Isaac. I feel like I've always known you.'

When he pulled her in closer, she knew he couldn't argue with her logic. There *was* some indescribable connection. They were strangers, because they'd only just met, yet it was as if they'd always known each other.

'I have no contraception, and I can't make love to you not knowing if you're on the Pill or use a coil or...'

'Shhhh. Just hold me.'

'There was nothing obvious in your handbag to indicate...'

'Don't say a word, Isaac,' she said, kissing him.

Isaac wondered if his hands would fall off. They felt so light, as if all the blood in his body rushed somewhere else, every time they touched her smooth and satiny skin.

'Liesel, you're not part of my life's plan. As soon as I can get an ambulance up here, or find a way to drive you to town myself, then we will part ways. It's not fair to make love to you… and then say goodbye. Not fair to either of us. And I can't bear the thought of you walking away, and never coming back.'

'What if I don't?'

'What if you don't *what*?' he asked in disbelief, knowing exactly what she was asking.

'Walk away. What if I stay?'

'You can't do that! You can't live with a man you don't know.'

'I do know you. I feel you in every part of my body, like electricity. It tingles, and snaps. It sizzles and pops. It's explosive. You can't really expect me to walk away knowing that neither of us will ever feel anything like this again in our lives. Can you?'

'You can't live in a remote castle in the Scottish highlands!'

'Why not? *You* do!'

'I'm a lot older than you, and I have no reason to be anywhere else!'

'You're only as old as the company you keep. Kiss me, Isaac. I know you want to.'

Who was this creature? She was enchanting and inviting. But more than anything, she was like a wild gypsy. There were no rules in her vocabulary. Isaac found himself tantalised and hopeful. Maybe there was more to life than looking across the loch and feeling sorry for himself? Remorse had etched itself deep into his jaded bones and he was weary of life; that much was true. Maybe it was time to stop living in his imagination and make things reality?

Liesel softly bit her bottom lip in anticipation. With a gentle growl, Isaac reached over and brushed his cheek against hers. Their lips met in a thrilling fusion. Finally, they were kissing. Tongues teasing each other, on a strident search for answers, wanting more; needing more from each other. Neither of them knew what it was beyond the passion. They were desperate to understand the complexities of their compelling and overwhelming attraction.

Isaac was stunned by the power of pleasure hurtling through his body, and he grew hungrier by the second. He couldn't have her begging. No, he'd pre-empt her every need. As Liesel moved her hips in closer to him, he sighed at the feel of her skin, her hair, her kisses. Isaac wanted more, and he wanted it now. There was nothing in the world more important than becoming one with her.

Isaac Heathfield: thirty-five years old, hermit, widower, and formerly miserable, was the happiest he'd ever been in living memory. And he was terrified of what that might mean. How could life change so quickly? In one day? Impossible! Perhaps this was all a dream, and he'd wake up soon.

'Make love to me, Isaac,' she said in the softest tone. 'I want to feel you inside me. Hold me close.'

Isaac held onto each word as she encouraged him to let go of his inhibitions.

'Show me how you feel. I know you want to. I can see it in your eyes. I've seen it there from the moment I met you. Don't resist this. It's real.'

With his hands either side of her shapely hips, he leant down to kiss her. 'I can do anything you want, but I can't go inside you. Not now. Not yet. Not until I know...'

Then he saw her face crumple. 'I'm not rejecting you, Liesel.' He tilted her sad face up so that their eyes met. 'I *want* to make love with you, but I can't...It would be irresponsible.' Right then and there he stopped talking. Words were useless. Instead, he wiped a tear from the corner of her eye. The last thing he wanted to do was upset her. What he really wanted was to make love with her, and never let her go. But that was ridiculous! Someone had to maintain some rational thinking around here. Just because they were in a castle it did not mean they lived in a fairytale! If there was anything that life had taught Isaac Heathfield, it was that there was no such thing as fairytales or happily ever afters. Not for him, anyway.

Isaac wiped her brow, and brushed off another tear.

Damn it. What choice did he have? To reject her would be to reject life itself! He kissed her soft cheek, and then her mouth. Their tongues danced a slow waltz, drawing each other closer, tempting, teasing and tantalising until there was no question that the dance would continue.

Isaac's hands moved down to her impressionable breasts; so soft and yielding. Kisses perched themselves upon each rising hot-pink nipple, and he watched them explode. Then, with his hands moving up under her shoulders, he eased himself inside. Slowly. Slowly. Slowly. When his breath caught, he realised he was terrified. Isaac had never wanted anything so badly in his life. Then and there he let himself go. There was no turning back now. And with each deep, penetrating movement, Liesel called out. At first, he wondered if he was hurting her, but her hands pushing firmly against his buttocks showed him that she wanted more of him. Unrestrained, he felt her urgency: deeper, fuller, closer.

As Isaac pushed himself further into her tender, receiving cavern, he was certain of one thing: he would never let her leave. The revelation shocked him to his core. What would this mean? He could hardly hold her captive.

Isaac caught another tear in the corner of her eye.

'Are you okay? Have I hurt you?' Isaac began to withdraw, a harsh betrayal of their comfortable and gentle rhythm.

'Don't do that. Stay inside me. I'm crying because...I've never felt so loved in my life.'

Isaac couldn't understand how a woman who had no idea who she was or anything about her life could say something like that.

'I feel it in every part of me. We're meant to be together. Stay inside me, Isaac.'

With gentle rocking and rhythmical movements, he guided her up, higher and higher, towards the pinnacle of pleasure. Her cries became louder, one after the other; insatiable, desperate for more of him. Together, their triumph called across the dark, starry, Scottish night.

Isaac stayed inside her for some time, their bodies collapsed; enmeshed, sated. If he could stay there forever, he would. When he was sure that she was asleep, he slowly withdrew, and lay back beside her.

It took him some time to surrender to the pull of sleep. Try as it might, it wasn't a powerful enough sedative to restrain the million thoughts racing around his head. Isaac never wanted her to leave, but he knew she had to. In a day or two, they'd be able to get past the storm damage and take her to the local hospital. In a day or two…the best thing that had ever happened to him, would walk away and his life would never be the same again. Why was life so consistently cruel to him? It wasn't like he was a bad person. He'd never hurt anyone! Not deliberately, anyway. He didn't deserve the pain of her walking away.

Isaac watched her breathing. Liesel looked so peaceful lying there in the dark, a hint of moonlight splashing across her skin. There was something so familiar about Liesel lying in his bed, sleeping serenely. It was as if she'd always been here. Peaceful she may be, he told himself, but it won't last. She has to go. And the sooner the better! Isaac despised the rollercoaster of emotions. Yes, no. Stay, go. Contentment, destruction. Enchantment, disillusionment. Why wasn't there some happy middle ground? Why was everything so black and white?

Liesel Eather wasn't the only one who seduced him that night. When sleep finally wrapped her tender arms around him, Isaac slept soundly: for the first time in ten years.

There were no nightmares, no screaming ghosts in the hallway. Just peace. Pure peace. And the promise of happier days to come. Lightning had transformed his life, and even if she left in the morning, one thing was for certain: his life would never be the same again. He'd been struck!

First light was always reluctant in January. It had to be dragged kicking and screaming over the horizon, and forced to confront the bleakness of Winter in Scotland.

Isaac awoke to the soft kisses of his lover: Liesel. She was smiling, and her slumberous eyes were filled with pleasure. Damn it! Why did she have to look like she belonged here?

Liesel was his lover. He was her lover.

He had a lover? Impossible! Isaac held her close, in awe of her beauty and laughter.

In the daylight, she looked even more gorgeous: her dark hair tousled around her slender, tanned shoulders; her smile welcoming him into consciousness. Her fingers saying 'Come to me, Isaac.'

Marvelling at her body—toned, yet soft in all the right places—Isaac observed her eyes: the shape of almonds; and her lashes were dark. He decided her smile was worth ten times the cost of his castle; she was priceless. And why, exactly, was he contemplating letting her walk away? Insane.

'More?' he asked, knowing exactly what she wanted. 'How can I resist you? I'm powerless against you.'

'I'll bet you've never felt more powerful in your life,' she giggled, teasing him with her finger across his unshaven jaw line.

'How do you figure that?'

'In fact, I'll bet you think you can take on the whole world this morning.'

And he found himself laughing in a way that he hadn't ever laughed before. She was right! How did she know him so well? Isaac liked how he felt when they were together. If he didn't know better, he'd think she was his missing half. It was a silly thought, though, and he dismissed it. This was the stuff of fairytales and romance novels, not real life. Such ideas were no part of his world.

'I think you might just be right!' He gently tickled her till she laughed, and then Liesel pushed him away from her, and onto his back. 'Stay there,' she said, and climbed on top of him.

The vision before Isaac nearly made him explode: she was straddled above, her round breasts ripe, and ready for his hands to reach up and hold. A soft, slow groan from deep within his belly left his lips.

'You're killing me, Liesel,' he said as he allowed himself to go deep into the centre of her being. One simple action had her calling out ecstatically across the grim and grey morning, the intensity of him pleasuring her so deeply was utterly overwhelming.

'You're wrong,' she laughed wickedly, bending forward to kiss him. 'You are so wrong. I'm bringing you back to life!'

And the truth of those words rammed a bolt of lighting right through him. Through both of them.

Life. He was alive.

'Did you *feel* that?' she gasped. 'Why does that keep happening to us?'

'Can you feel *this*?' he asked as he thrust himself deeper inside her, trying to distract Liesel from the electricity; trying to distract himself. There was a truth to her words that he didn't want to acknowledge.

Whatever it was that brought them together, it was going to have to be an equally powerful force that pulled them apart. They both knew that.

They circled the summit of intense pleasure until they could stand it no longer, beckoning each other over, over, over until they tumbled, stumbled, exhausted, expired, entranced, right back to the place where they started. Words had no place in their lives right now. Instead, they held each other for the longest time, gazing into each other's eyes, smiling. Kissing. Wrapped in a cocoon away from the world, they were one.

Calling Home

'But I don't want you to phone the Australian embassy, Isaac. I don't care where I'm from. My past is irrelevant. All that matters is us, right here, right now: just the two of us. Don't do this. Don't send me away. It's wrong!'

Liesel was wearing one of Isaac's shirts, and thick woollen socks, as she padded about on the solid-oak floorboards of his bedroom, gripping her arms and shivering from the cold.

'Someone will be looking for you. There'll be people worried about you. I'm virtually holding you hostage. It's a mistake on so many levels that I've got you here.'

'What if I don't want to go? Doesn't that mean anything?' Defiant, with her hands on her hips and a scowl on her face, it was all Isaac could do not to laugh out loud.

'What's so funny?'

'You! You're so gorgeous. Look at you standing there,' he laughed. 'I still can't believe how you burst into my life and captivated me even before you opened your eyes.'

'And that's *funny*?' she asked, incredulous that he wasn't honouring the gravity of their dilemma. And it was *their* dilemma. She knew, without doubt, that he didn't want her to leave.

'No. You, standing there in my shirt and socks, demanding I keep you prisoner here till the end of your days.'

'I don't see the funny side. I don't want to leave you. And I can't believe you want me to go.'

'I don't! Of course I don't want you to leave. But we both have lives to lead. What we've got...it can't go on.' Isaac turned away. It was unbearable looking in her tear-filled eyes, knowing the pain he was causing. 'I'm sorry.'

'Damn it, Isaac. Are you always so stubborn?' She asked, pulling him to face her.

His only response was to raise his eyebrows. Liesel wasn't the first woman who'd called him that, but he found himself hoping she'd be the last, even if it meant she'd call him stubborn for the next fifty years.

'Go back to bed. We'll talk about this later when you're calmer,' he insisted. Isaac was in no mood to argue with a volatile force of nature.

'No! We'll talk about it now. I don't want to leave. You can't make me leave. What are you going to do? Carry me out of here and dump me at the bottom of the driveway?'

'Are you always so dramatic? On second thoughts, don't answer that.'

'How would I know what I am? I don't know *who* I am. All I know is that with you I feel real. I feel like a woman. Don't take that away from me, Isaac. Please.'

Vulnerability swept across her features, and he couldn't bear it. What happened to the feisty bold Australian girl who stole his heart? Right now she looked terrified. Frightened for her life. Isaac knew exactly how she felt.

'I promise I'm not going to dump you anywhere. You have my word. But…but I can't *not* make contact with the outside world. I have a duty to inform the authorities that you're safe. If I could wrap us up in a bubble for the rest of our lives, then I most certainly would.'

The words coming out of his mouth startled him. Was he just promising her marriage? A lifetime of fidelity? How long had he known her? Isaac shook his head in disbelief.

'Don't phone anyone, Isaac,' she begged. 'It will be the end of us if you do.'

Moved by her vulnerability, he immediately wrapped his arms around her.

'I love you,' she whispered, her words rushing through his heart like warm Summer wind.

I love you, too, he thought to himself. And words he never thought he'd utter in his life, came spinning into his mind like it was the most natural thing in the world. He could have kicked himself for such carelessness thinking. *I love you too!* When did this happen? Lightning, how did this happen? Isaac was grateful not to have shared his thoughts out loud. There was no way she'd leave if he declared what had just gone through his mind. Isaac wrapped his arms around her, desperate to keep hold of her, and yet wrestling with his conscience.

'If there is any part of you that loves me too, then don't do this. I'm begging you, Isaac. I'm scared.' Tears slid down her cheeks.

'I know you are.' Isaac caught her tears, and held her close.

What the hell was he going to do with her? As he listened to the chattering of her teeth, he said 'We need to get you some warmer clothes. Your body isn't designed for this climate. Come with me.'

Isaac led her down the long hallway, to the far end of the castle. Liesel had only been in her bedroom and bathroom, and hadn't given any thought to how vast his home was until she walked by room after room.

The huge paintings must have been Isaac's ancestors, she decided, and then she paused by a window to take in the view. The loch was surrounded by frozen fields and hills.

'This is so beautiful. It's utterly breathtaking. I can see why you live here.'

'Yes, it is.'

Looking curiously over towards the driveway at half of a yellow VW, defiantly holding its ground against a huge tree trunk, she gasped.

'Is that the car I was driving?' It was obvious that the fact she was standing and looking at the remains of it was nothing short of a miracle.

'What's left of it, yes.'

'And I'm alive?'

'A miracle, if ever there was one,' he said, catching his breath.

'A miracle? No, Isaac; it's destiny.' She took his hand as they walked further down the long hall. 'Can't you see? We're meant to be together.'

No, Isaac didn't want to see. Damn it, they weren't meant to be together. She shouldn't even be here.

'What is a miracle is that your car even got up the hill. According to the paperwork in the glove box, it would appear you bought it in Germany rather cheaply. It should have gone to the scrap heap, not the car yard.'

'It's not the car's fault that I'm here,' she smirked. 'It's destiny.'

Isaac kissed her on the forehead noting that she was pretty cute when she wasn't yelling.

At the end of the hallway, he slowed down. Isaac opened the door, and tentatively looked inside.

Liesel wasn't sure what he was looking for, but it was as if he expected someone to be in there. When he seemed certain that it was empty, he led her inside.

'Whose bedroom is this?' she asked, taking in the sight of old perfume bottles and ruffled pink cushions scattered across the bed and chaise longue. Long velvet curtains matched the bedcover, and were the same fuchsia colour as the rugs.

'My late wife's room.' He said it as a statement of fact, rather than with a sense of loyalty or sadness or sentiment.

'You were *married*!'

The way she hurled those words so violently at him kicked Isaac in the guts. It was as if he'd committed a crime which had left Liesel devastated. Why on Earth was she reacting like this?

'Married?' she asked again, shaking her head in disbelief.

'Yes, I was.' Isaac opened the door of a large oak wardrobe trying not to buy into her melodramatic performance. 'You may as well put these clothes to good use.'

'You want me to wear your *wife's* clothes? I can't believe what you're asking of me!' Liesel's hands were on her hips, and he was sure he saw her stamp her foot.

'She's not my wife now. The clothes are of no use to me, but they'll sure as hell keep you warm,' he said, wondering what he could do to placate her anger.

'No.'

'What do you mean, "no"?' He tried to stay calm. Why was she being so difficult? And why was "no" her most used word?

'Why are you only just telling me that you're married!'

'*Was* married. I'm not married now. What are you so angry about?'

'I can't bear the thought of you being with another woman! That's what I'm angry about.' Liesel said as she paced the room, jealousy raging from her very bones.

Isaac couldn't understand her logic. How could she be furious about a decision he'd made more than a decade ago? Surely she was being unreasonable.

'I married Marylynn eleven years ago. This weekend marked the tenth anniversary of her death. I hardly think she's competition for you, Liesel. Now, choose some clothes. I can't stand to see you shivering.' But he had no idea that her goose bumps were of fear, not from the harsh Scottish Winter which had gripped the castle with its relentless pincer grip.

'Fine!' she snapped. 'Just fine. I'll wear her damn clothes. But you better not think of her when you see me wearing them, or I'll....'

'*That* would be an impossibility. You're nothing alike at all.' He said, and dipped his head so that she didn't see the faint smile on his lips. He couldn't help it. Even when she was raging with fury, she was adorable and so passionate. So alive. And that was what had been missing in his life for all these years. Isaac wasn't going to tell her that, though. That would be exactly the lifeline she was looking for to anchor herself into his life.

He watched her search through the wardrobe, and in the chest of drawers.

Liesel was frowning. 'Why have you kept these clothes for all these years?'

'I don't have an answer for that. Maybe I knew you were coming, and that you'd need some clothes,' he smiled, hoping to appeal to the part of her which sensed a deeper mystery to their connection. It was a mystery which defied logic.

Liesel slipped into a pair of maroon corduroy trousers, and matching long-sleeved shirt and cardigan. 'They don't smell like they've been sitting in drawers for ten years.'

'Adalene comes through and cleans everything from time to time, including the clothing. Take whatever else you want, and then we don't have to come back to this room.'

'You're a strange man, Isaac Heathfield. I love you, but I'm not entirely sure I understand you.'

Stubborn. Strange. What next?

'Any more compliments that you want to throw my way?' he laughed, thinking that she looked like she might be on the verge of forgiving him for doing something so thoughtless as marrying another woman.

'You're terribly handsome.' Liesel stood back and looked at him quite seriously. 'I love the way your dark hair tries to curl, but sort of gives up on itself and sits in little helpless waves instead. Your hair is the colour of the unlit night sky, and can't decide if it's black, ebony, sable or coal. And those dimples when you smile. I melt every time. Do you know that? I love your teeth: so strong, so white; and your jawline: it's stronger than a castle wall. It tells me you're a man of strength, of character; that you won't be defeated. Your mouth just begs for me to kiss you,' she whispered, kissing him lightly. And then she held her fingers softly against the side of his eyes. 'And those little lines there, they tell me you need to laugh more. I want to see those lines grow. Your muscles make me swoon. I love how you smell of coffee. There's something so incredibly sexy about your seriousness, but when you smile or laugh, I'm lost. I just tip over the edge. I'm enchanted. If there is such a thing as a slow espresso, then that's what you are: deep, strong, addictive, and the smallest sip satiates. But, you know, you're just so devastatingly handsome that no matter what you do, I'm captivated. Lucky for you, or I might not have stayed.'

'So you're only with me for my good looks then? And here I was thinking it was my Scottish charm.'

Liesel laughed out loud. 'I'm sorry for being so crabby. I can't explain why I felt so jealous. I am sorry. I don't know what came over me.'

'Liesel, there is nothing for you to be jealous of. I can promise you that.'

'I...' she looked down at her sock-covered feet, 'can't stand the thought of you loving another woman; loving anyone else but me.'

Isaac moved in closer to her, and lifted her chin up with his fingers. When their eyes met, lightning struck. They both lost their balance. 'I never loved Marylynn. I liked her, and I hoped it would grow into love, but it didn't.'

Liesel pulled away. 'How could you marry someone you didn't love?'

Here we go again, he thought. She's back to being feisty, bossy, demanding. It was like living in the midst of an electrical storm.

'Come to the kitchen, and I'll make us some food. And if you're really that interested, I'll tell you all about it.'

They held hands as they walked down two flights of stairs. A chill wind followed them.

'Is this place always so cold?' she asked, rubbing her hands up and down her arms.

'It's about thirty-degrees Celsius colder than what

you'll be used to, judging by the colour of your skin. I'm surprised you haven't died of hypothermia!'

Isaac got sidetracked and gave Liesel a tour around most of the castle, apart from his study and other private rooms. Stoneyhill Castle was built in the mid-15th century, and had a four-story tower. A vaulted room led through into the open courtyard. The tower house had the best views, as did one of the turrets overlooking the loch; the water was an important reserve for waterfowl. Liesel took in the sight of the jetty, and the shoreline where mudflats and sandy beaches provided a boggy ground for local wildlife. On from that it led to the tussocky ground near the river, and beyond to the woods.

'This is called a tower-house castle, and was considerably expensive to build. The original building was centred around the tower, with the great halls, kitchens and stables originally made from wood.'

'I keep trying to find words to describe this place, Isaac: mysterious, formidable, magnificent, intriguing. But none of them do it justice. Stoneyhill is so compelling.'

Isaac wrapped a jacket around Liesel's shoulders, and they stepped outside into the grounds which were designed as a grand park. Oak trees and Scots pine dotted the landscaped gardens. Most of the young plants were buried beneath ice and snow.

Liesel shivered against the cold, and standing a few hundred metres back from the castle, she marvelled at the way it was perched on a spur of volcanic rock, against a backdrop of snowy mountains. 'In the Summer, those glens are covered in purple and mauve heather,' Isaac said, as if remembering something pleasant.

'You really love this place, don't you?' she said, holding his hand tightly.

'I didn't, at first, but it grew on me as season after season I found its treasures to be inspiring and mesmerising. Nature is a worthy companion.'

They returned to the side entrance, and Isaac pointed out a wall of note. 'It's 16-feet wide here, and that wall there is 60-feet high.'

'Yeah, it must be, I've just cricked my neck!' she laughed.

'Let's get you inside, and out of the cold. The Sun will be down anytime from now.'

The kitchen was vast, and the walls were lined with oak dressers; and a large wooden table, obviously set for household staff, was laid out with plates, glasses and cutlery. Isaac searched the fridge, and rummaged through the pantry.

'I'd love a mango,' Liesel said quietly. 'I really feel like eating one.'

Isaac looked at her seriously. 'You're in Scotland, not Australia. There are no mangos here.'

'Oh, well, what fruit do you have?'

'In January? Nothing. He went to the deep freezer, and pulled out a bag of raspberries. 'This is the closest you'll get to fruit around here. I'm sorry.'

They ate a simple meal of sourdough rye bread, apple and raspberry chutney, Ayrshire cheese, and shared a bottle of red wine. Isaac watched the way she ate. Perhaps they didn't use cutlery in Australia, he thought more than once as she licked her fingers, and moaned with pleasure as she made her way through no less than four thick slices of bread. Isaac wasn't sure he'd ever met anyone so sensual. Everything about Liesel Eather was refreshing: she was like Summer sunshine spread across a bleak Winter's day, melting everything in sight, including his heart.

Listening to her gently moan as she made food noises, brought back memories of their lovemaking. It was all he could do to contain himself and concentrate on his sandwich. Everything about her aroused him. Each minute with her rendered him senseless. She, and she alone, made him glad to be alive. Isaac couldn't remember ever experiencing this before in his life.

'My staff members are due back tomorrow morning. I'm not entirely sure they'll get through if the trees haven't been removed. It will feel different around here when they're back. You'll need to prepare yourself for that. It won't be just you and I anymore.'

'Why do you need them? What do they do that you can't do for yourself?' she asked matter of factly.

'Nothing, probably, but I have work to do and it makes my life easier if there are people to cook, clean, garden, run errands and so on.'

'I can run errands for you,' she offered with great enthusiasm. 'And I can cook, clean, and if the Sun ever comes out, I could grow vegetables.'

Isaac adored her passion. Was it passion, though, or desperation? Either way, the thought of her being around and wanting to look after him made his heart joyful.

'You will go back to your life soon, Liesel. When your memory returns, you'll walk away. You'll probably be disgusted that you even slept with me!'

'That would never be true! How can you say that?' And once again, she was fuming.

Liesel ran back to the bedroom, and fell on the bed sobbing her heart out. How could he even suggest

61

that they part? It was crazy! They were destined to be together, now and always. Why would Isaac say that she would change her mind about him? Impossible! She loved everything about him, even his uptight British habits. They were endearing in a strange sort of way.

Isaac followed her up to the bedroom. He should have known better than to say anything like that, but he wanted her to face up to reality. Things *were* going to change. They couldn't pretend otherwise. He sat beside her on the bed, softly stroking her head. 'I'm sorry.'

'Stop pushing me away, Isaac. Why are you doing that? Stop resisting what we have.'

Isaac was lost for words. Nothing about them being together made sense, and yet the idea of turning her away and never seeing her again made even less sense.

As he sat patiently, his eyes caught sight of the violin on the other side of the room. Not once had she expressed interest in it.

'Play your violin for me, Liesel,' he asked.

'I don't know how to play,' she replied solemnly.

'I don't believe that. It was in your car. The books inside have your name in them. They're advanced manuscripts. Your brain will remember how to play.'

'I don't know anything about my life; I'm hardly capable of playing an instrument!'

Isaac moved away from her, and lifted the violin case onto the bed then he carefully opened it, and removed the fine instrument from the midnight-blue velvet-lined casing. Isaac estimated the violin to be about three hundred years old, and quite valuable.

Isaac passed her the violin, and she tentatively held it in her hands. Liesel reached for the bow, and instinctively tightened the fine horse-hair strings.

'How did you know to do that?' Isaac asked.

'Do what?' she asked him.

'Tighten the bow.'

'Oh. I don't know.'

Liesel stood up, and lifted the violin to her chin, and raised the bow above her head.

'Your posture is amazing,' he whispered.

Within seconds she began to play Johann Strauss's *The Blue Danube*.

Instantly, Isaac was transported by the gliding of her bow.

The musical passages took him on a journey, moving him towards something, and then away. He let himself experience the change in tempos, and how the music invited him to places unknown.

Minutes later, she put the violin back in its case. 'Must be a fluke or something. I don't know how to play a violin!'

Isaac put his arms around her. Tears choked his eyes. The wall between who she was with him, and the person she was on the other side of that storm-damaged oak tree, seemed light years away.

'You're a virtuoso, Liesel. There was nothing fluke-like about that playing.'

'Take it away. I don't want to see that thing again!'

'Liesel, what are you talking about? You have a gift. To play an instrument like that takes years and years of work and dedication. You mastered your craft. I'm not taking it away, but I sure as hell am going to start making some phone calls.'

'No! You promised, Isaac.'

'I promised I wouldn't send you away, and I won't. But I can't keep you holed up here in an ancient castle,' he said. 'If nothing else, you'd die of hypothermia.

Your body isn't designed for this weather.'

Isaac crawled in bed beside her as she lay weeping. 'I don't want to let you go, but I can't hide you here forever. People will be looking for you. It's not right. The last thing I want is to have this place crawling with police, or have the media camped out on my doorstep!'

For the longest time he held her in his arms. The weight of the future lay before them.

Isaac tried to convince himself that all he felt was lust; that it was impossible to fall in love so quickly, and to want to devote and dedicate your life to another in such a short space of time. It was *impossible*! The truth was that he was a virile man with strong urges that had been suppressed for way too long. Everything about Liesel Eather gave him permission to feel again. He mustn't confuse lust with anything long term or sustainable.

When she eventually fell asleep, Isaac tiptoed down the corridor to make some phone calls. Firstly he contacted the Australian embassy in London, then, as an impromptu idea, phoned the village pub.

'Funnily enough,' the landlord's thick Scottish brogue came down the line, 'there's a young man here who's been looking for a wee Australian lass. Leez, he calls her. Dark brown hair, five foot eight, small nose? They were meant to meet here a couple of days ago, and he's beside himself with worry. I'll send him up your way, Mr Heathfield, first thing in the morning.'

'Thank you, Douglas. I'll be waiting for him.'

Isaac's heart sank. Of course there was a man! There was no way on this Earth that Liesel would be single. Women like her weren't designed to be alone. No, they were made to be held, loved, longed for, cherished and desired.

Isaac had to warn her, and he had to brace himself for the fact that, no matter how much he wanted it to be otherwise, she'd be leaving him for good. Isaac paced the front reception area. How was he going to tell Liesel? She'd be incandescent with rage. He could see it now: She'd say 'No!' She'd stamp her feet, and shake her finger at him; a tempestuous toddler in the body of a beautiful woman. And when he thought of that body, and what he'd be giving up, he wanted to beat the door down.

Life was good before she came along, wasn't it, Isaac? He asked himself this several times, before muttering that things could finally go back to normal when she left. Who was he kidding? In just a few short days his whole life had been transformed. Did he really want to give this up? Was he really prepared to go back to "same old, same old" when he could have this? He cursed. What choice did he have? It wasn't his choice to make!

The next morning, he awoke ridiculously early and paced the kitchen. Not even the freshly brewed coffee tempted him. The moment of truth: would Liesel choose Isaac or her fiancé? Was there even a choice to make? And if she did choose to stay, what sense would that even make? It didn't! They knew nothing about each other, or their lives. It was wrong to even contemplate such a scenario. Isaac put his thoughts into check. There was no decision to make. Liesel had to leave, and Isaac would just have to live with the fact that the woman who enchanted him so much was *not* destined to be part of his life any longer.

Isaac spied a lone figure, sporting a heavy backpack, trekking up the driveway towards Stoneyhill Castle. The person stopped several times to take photos of the castle, and of the loch below. The five-minute walk up the hill took him forty-five minutes. It occurred to Isaac that the man should have been more interested in seeing Liesel than taking photos. Where were his priorities? Isaac couldn't reconcile the lackadaisical figure with the frantic guy the publican spoke of.

Isaac thought better of waking Liesel to warn her, and instead would wait to see if she recognised the man.

The loud bell at the front door of Stoneyhill Castle echoed through the parklands. Winter bent over backwards with the acoustics; after all, she had nothing else to do on such a sour morning.

'A visitor?' Liesel thought to herself as she sat upright in bed, rubbing her eyes. She wandered down the hall and two flights of stairs to find Isaac. Curiosity led her towards him. Not once had he mentioned that there'd be visitors. Maybe it was his staff returning to work. In a moment of glee, she couldn't wait to meet them all.

Isaac answered the front door, with his chest pounding like muffled percussion, labouring under a bucket of emotional concrete. He'd dreaded this moment.

What sort of man was Liesel attracted to? And more importantly, was he good enough for her? Would she leave at the very moment she saw her boyfriend? Would she be filled with regret for sleeping with Isaac? That their time together might not mean anything to her was an unbearable thought for Isaac.

'G'day mate, I'm Duncan Trantor,' he said, identifying himself with a broad Australian accent. 'I believe my fiancée, Liesel Eather, is a guest of yours?' The upward inflections in his voice made Isaac's skin crawl. One look at his messy sandy-blond hair and he figured the guy was a surfer.

'Isaac Heathfield,' he said politely, reaching out his hand to shake Duncan's.

'Yes, she's staying here. I think there's something you should know. She was in an accident.'

'That car down the driveway? Under the tree? Mate,' he said in a thick, lazy drawl; an accent that wasn't in a hurry. 'How did she get out of there alive? Is she hurt?'

'Physically, she's just fine. But she's lost her memory.'

'What? *All* of it?' He laughed. For some reason, the idea of it amused, rather than concerned, him.

'Yes. She doesn't know who she is, or anything about her life.'

'She'll remember me!' Duncan laughed. 'We're getting married in a fortnight.'

Isaac immediately disliked his cocky attitude. *Married?* Did he hear that right? No! What a nightmare. Isaac couldn't let it happen.

This man was all wrong for Liesel. And then he mentally kicked himself. How the hell would he know who was right or wrong for her? He didn't even know her.

Maybe Isaac was all wrong for Liesel! And that was the truth: he didn't know Liesel Eather. Well, he knew her in a biblical sense, but he didn't know her in any meaningful way like this fiancé of hers did.

'Follow me,' he said, and as he turned, Isaac saw Liesel coming down the staircase wearing his late wife's red-tartan pyjamas and matching red slippers.

The whole situation seemed surreal. His past, her past, the present...*and what of the future?* What would happen to them? Isaac had no way to warn her, or protect her from what was about to happen.

'Babe,' Duncan called out, racing up to greet her, his arms outstretched.

'Get off me!' she yelled when he hugged her.

'Isaac. Who is this person?' She asked helplessly.

Duncan backed away. 'Babe? It's me. You remember me. I'm your fiancé. Duncan. Remember, you've been travelling around Europe. We were going to have a week's holiday here in the Highlands, and then home to Australia to get married. You can't have forgotten that! Our back-to-front honeymoon, we called it. Pleasure, then work. Afterwards, you're going on your concert tour.'

The panicked expression on her face made Isaac's heart pound. If he could, he'd lift her up in his arms and carry her away; far, far away.

'Isaac, I don't know who this man is. Please make him go.' Tears slipped from her eyes.

'Babe, it's me. Of course you remember me!' Duncan laughed, thinking it was all a bit of a joke, with no idea of the ramifications her amnesia would have on his life. On all of their lives.

'He's right, Liesel.' Isaac spoke slowly, more to keep himself calm than to reassure her. 'Duncan has come looking for you. To take you home.' The words ripped through his gut like a demon. It was unthinkable that they could be torn apart.

'No!' She strode up the staircase two at a time, and repeated her mantra on every step. 'No. No. No. No.'

'I'm sorry, Duncan. She's going to need some time to come around to the idea. We can't force this on her.'

'Well how long's that gonna take, mate? We've got a wedding in two weeks!' he asked, exasperated at this change of plans. It's been bad enough that she left me to do all the planning.'

'I can't answer that. I don't know how long this will last. As soon as we can get that tree cleared from the driveway, then I'll bring a consultant in. You're welcome to stay here tonight, but you need to give her space and time. She's vulnerable right now.' Isaac spoke firmly, trying not to give away his feelings for her. It would be disastrous for Duncan to discover that Liesel was making love with Isaac.

They walked up the staircase, and Isaac knocked on her door.

'Liesel, may we come in?' Isaac asked. 'Liesel?'

There was no answer, so he gently pushed the door open. She was lying, face down, on the bed, crying.

'Liesel, let Duncan talk. It might help jog your memory. I'll leave you to it, but I won't be far away if you need me.'

When she looked up at him, with terror in her eyes, it made it that much harder for Isaac to walk away.

'Babe...'

'Don't call me babe!' she yelled at him furiously. Liesel stomped around the room, trying to find the power within her to deal with this stranger. Finally, she sat on the bed.

Despite the gravity of the situation, Isaac couldn't help smile. Duncan had his work cut out. Isaac decided to stand just outside the door. It was wrong to eavesdrop on a couple who were about to get married—his stomach lurched at the thought of her being with Duncan—but he decided to listen anyway.

'Alright. Stop being so angry with me. You're not an angry person. You're always so calm and chilled.' He walked over and sat on the bed.

'*Don't* sit on this bed. I don't know you. And I don't want you anywhere near me. Why are you here? Did I ask you to come here? No, I didn't.'

Duncan breathed deeply trying to keep calm, then he stood up and paced the room. Every inch of him strained to be mature, civil and patient; but he failed.

'What sort of game is this, Liesel? What more do you want from me? I've given you everything you asked for! I know you said you needed space, but surely a four-month expedition across Europe was plenty of space?'

'I don't want anything from you. You can leave. I don't know you. I don't feel anything when I look at you. Surely if you were important to me then I'd feel something, even if I don't remember it?'

Liesel was adamant that he was nothing more than a stranger. 'You could be any old person off the street. Am I just supposed to take your word for it that we're due to be married, and then walk away with you?'

Duncan was unable to contain his anger, and began to yell.

'You know, if you weren't so insistent about staying a virgin till your wedding night you'd probably remember who I was! It would be in your bones!' he shouted, angrily pacing the room. 'But no, every time I tried to even put my hand under your blouse you'd protest. Some rot about lovemaking being sacred, and that you wanted to wait until the time was right. You're not even religious, but you damn well acted like a nun! Perhaps we should have sex right now, and then you'd know who you were! You'd certainly know who I was!'

Isaac nearly lost his balance. *Virgin? Till her wedding night?* Not only had he made love to Duncan's fiancée, he'd also taken her virginity. His mind raced back to the first time they made love. Nothing, nothing at all, led him to believe it was her first time. Just remembering her moans and delighted whimpers made him weak at the knees. Isaac felt his arousal begin. *Not now*, he scolded. He wondered, for just a moment, if Liesel would confess to their relationship, and he listened as his heart thudded, like the ominous drums of a battle march. If he was honest with himself, he didn't entirely trust Liesel not to say anything, given how tempestuous she could be. Right now she was a loose cannon, and he wasn't entirely sure that he wanted to witness any explosions she triggered.

'Don't you dare even think of touching me. I don't remember who I was, and what I did or didn't do. I have no idea what you're talking about. I really wish you'd leave me alone. Go back to Australia and find someone new, because I'm *not* going back. Ever.'

'I'm not taking no for an answer. You've no idea how worried I was about you when you didn't turn up at the pub. I thought you'd died. I'm not walking away Liesel, even if I have to wait fifty years for your memory to return. I'll make you love me. I'll do whatever it takes!'

'No. You can't make me.'

'When did you become so…stubborn? You were always so malleable!'

'I don't know who I was, so stop speaking to me about that person. It's meaningless to me. I'm not marrying you. I'm not going back to Australia.'

'What about your concerts?'

'What concerts? I don't even play an instrument! Leave me alone. I want Isaac. Find me Isaac. Now!'

At the mention of his name, Isaac disappeared down the hallway so that Duncan wouldn't know he'd been listening.

'Ring that damn bell. I'm sure he'll come running.' Duncan said in disgust.

Liesel rang the bell as if her life depended on it.

Duncan paced back and forward, glaring at Liesel. 'How the hell did this happen? We're meant to be getting married, and you're living here like some wounded princess! I'm not happy. I'm not happy at all. I want to get you on the first plane back home. Let's call our Scottish holiday off, and just focus on the wedding and concerts.'

'Isaac. I want Duncan to leave,' she insisted when he entered the bedroom.

'He's concerned about you, Liesel. He can stay here tonight, and we'll see how you feel in the morning.'

The hollow look on her face mirrored his feelings. He felt her eyes searching his for answers, reassurance, hope. If Duncan stayed the night, there was no way Isaac and Liesel could share a bed. Emptiness swirled around their hearts, haunting their blossoming love. If there was anything they could do at this very moment it would be to wrap their arms around each other. It felt like torture to be so close, but unable to feel each other's breaths, or be enveloped in the warmth of their skin.

'Even if we postpone the wedding, we have to go back for the concerts. Thousands of people have paid to come and watch you play. You can't let them down.'

'If I was dead they wouldn't be able to see me

perform. Just tell them I'm dead! You hear me, tell them I'm dead! *I'm dead!* That life is gone. It's over.'

Duncan looked at Isaac, hoping for solidity and advice.

'I don't play the violin, do I Isaac?' she asked, desperate for him to back her up.

Was she asking him to lie for her?

'Why the hell were you travelling with a violin?' Duncan yelled.

'Duncan, she needs to rest. I'll show you to your room.' Isaac tried to stay calm, and left the bedroom.

Duncan followed him down the hallway, and Isaac led him to a guest room in another wing; that way, he wouldn't be able to hear any conversations that Liesel and Isaac had, but while he was on the property it wouldn't be wise for Isaac to stay in her room. Damn it!

Duncan looked around the spacious apartment. It was larger than his house. Tastefully decorated in maroons, and ebony black, he was taken by surprise at the opulence of this isolated castle.

'I appreciate what you're doing for her, mate, but I think I should just take her home. I don't think it's helping her to stay here pretending her old life doesn't exist.'

'She's not pretending.' Isaac was furious, but kept his emotions under control. His voice remained calm and even. Thirteen years in England's most renowned boarding school had taught him just where to shove any uncomfortable feelings, and how to show a dignified front. By the time he was six years of age, he'd excelled at the skill. Isaac had learnt, over the course of his first year, that no one was going to come and rescue him from the pain of being separated from his home and family. No one at all. Life showed him in no uncertain terms that the only person you could rely on was yourself.

'You should find everything you need in this room. Make yourself comfortable.' Isaac turned to walk away, leaving Duncan to fend on his own.

'Adalene, the maid, will bring a meal later,' Isaac said. 'It's best if you dine alone. Liesel needs space.'

When Isaac entered Liesel's room, she ran into his arms.

'You have got to stop being so mean to him,' he whispered into her hair. 'He loves you, and he's concerned.'

'You love me, Isaac. I can feel it in every part of my body. I don't feel that from him. It's...it's as if...I can't find the words.'

'It's only because you don't remember him. It will come back to you.'

'No, it's not that...'

Isaac sensed her confusion. Words might come later, but first she needed Isaac to kiss her. And kiss her, he did. Isaac held her so tenderly, that he almost thought she was going to break in his arms. More fragile than a china doll, he caressed her until she was able to breathe more steadily.

'Never let me go,' she whispered, her voice trembling. 'Never. I belong with you.'

Isolation

As Isaac, Duncan and Liesel sat around the kitchen table, the tension in the air felt thicker than the relentless January fog.

'Mr Heathfield, if you don't mind me asking, what do you do up here all day in this castle? Doesn't it get lonely? I mean, it's so far away from *everything*.'

Isaac had many opportunities to correct Duncan, and insist he call him Isaac, but for some reason he didn't. Perhaps he wanted the cocky young Australian to know just who ran this damn castle. The ancient building hadn't been in his family for centuries for no reason. The Heathfield clan was strong and proud, and damn it, they'd earned their respect.

'Loneliness is not something I suffer from. I like my own company.'

Duncan snickered 'You sound like Liesel. That's what she always says.'

Isaac and Liesel looked at each other. Lightning flashed through the air.

Duncan baulked at the feeling in his gut, but wasn't quite sure what it was. For an odd moment, he felt as if Liesel was in a relationship with Heathfield rather than still being his fiancée.

Odd, he thought. He brushed the feeling aside. What a ridiculous idea. Of course nothing had happened between them. Liesel wasn't a two-timer!

'It's not natural for humans to be alone. We're social animals,' he said. When neither of them said anything, he continued: 'So, babe…er, Liesel,' Duncan said, pulling a piece of paper from his backpack. 'This is the brochure of your concert tour.'

Duncan passed her the piece of paper so she could read through it.

'I don't know who this person is, and I don't play the violin. You can't make me go.'

'I'll bet you could play if you just picked it up. I'm sure it would all come back to you. Can't you even try?'

'I think you need to accept the fact that Liesel doesn't feel connected to that part of herself,' Isaac said calmly.

Duncan grabbed the paper from her, and passed it to Isaac. He read through it.

Liesel Eather makes her debut concert tour spanning Melbourne, Sydney, Adelaide, Auckland and Brisbane. Still relatively unknown, Ms Eather has been described as the virtuoso of her generation.

Isaac looked at her, and tried to imagine her playing in front of crowds of people.

'Duncan, answer me this: if Liesel says she likes her own company, and tends towards being a loner, how come she is set to play before huge crowds of people?'

'Because...' Duncan wasn't sure how to answer the question. 'Her music teacher believes it is something she needs to do.'

'So it's not Liesel's choice?'

'I wouldn't get all psychological about it!' Duncan was frustrated by the situation. 'Liesel's talented. If you heard her play, you'd understand. She's worked too hard not to do this.'

Isaac shot Liesel a quick glance.

'That's not really the point. If she doesn't like crowds, and prefers to be alone, then maybe concerts aren't the best idea. Just because someone's a musician, it doesn't automatically mean they're a performer. There is a world of difference.'

'Mate, you don't know Liesel. I do! She's a calm person; not cranky and like she is here. She might like her own company, but she could easily pull off this tour.'

'Stop talking about me like I'm not in the room!' Liesel cried out. She raced out of the kitchen, and up the staircase.

'Duncan, have you been in touch with her parents?'

'Parents? Hasn't she told you?'

'Duncan, she hasn't told me anything! Remember, she's lost her memory? She didn't even know her name.'

'Oh, yeah.'

Isaac couldn't comprehend how the Liesel he knew would want to marry such an *idiot*. Quite quickly, he was beginning to lose sympathy for Duncan's plight.

'They died when she was about fifteen. In a car accident, as it happens. This is a bit spooky, now that I come to think about it. Lightning struck a tree, and...'

'You're joking, right?' Isaac's head spun.

'Cut the car right in half, with them underneath it. The weird thing is she's never been scared of lightning, even after that tragic event. She'll often stand in a thunderstorm as if...well, it's like she's trying to be struck by lightning herself. You know, her dad used to call her Lightning. Drove her mother crazy; she always said it was asking for trouble. I don't think she has a death wish, it's more that she's trying to defy the laws of nature. I've never understood it myself. She thinks something life-changing will happen if she gets struck by lightning. Liesel doesn't seem to factor in that the bloody thing could kill her!'

'Who looked after her? How did she get over it?' Isaac wanted to hold her. He knew the pain of losing your parents.

'An aunt. Aunt Bess. She died last year. Brain tumour. Real sad it was, too. Bess helped her with the violin though, and made sure she got the best teachers. She even sold Liesel's parents' home so she could fund lessons, and get her the best instrument. Liesel was going to give up playing when her parents died. They were on their way to see her give a solo performance at a music festival. She searched for them in the audience and couldn't see them anywhere, but Liesel won the festival with a distinction anyway. She could have begun her career right then and there. But when the news was broken to her, and the realisation that they'd not even seen her perform...well, she insisted that she was never going to play again. As I say, Bess got her back on track. She didn't take no for an answer. And trust me, Leez is the Queen of No when she doesn't want to do something. Bess made her play for hours every day.'

'That's a lot of grief in one person's life.' Isaac forced himself to take deep breaths, to restrain the rising emotion before it overwhelmed him, and kept his back to Duncan for some time while he stared out the window.

'She shied away from public performances. She said she was too scared to shine, and perhaps people wouldn't come to see her; that—and I know this sounds stupid—maybe something bad would happen to them and they'd die before they got to the venue.'

'It doesn't sound stupid.' Isaac knew exactly what it felt like to hide your light away for fear of ridicule or rejection.

'There was the hypnosis, she tried, and it helped a bit, both with her grief, and also with performing. Her parents had one of those marriages: they were desperately in love with each other. Love at first sight, or some rubbish. Liesel said that's what she wanted in life: an all-consuming love. That was all she wanted. I offered her a happily ever after.'

'Did you love her? Is it what you wanted?'

'What do you mean? Love is overrated. We were friends. I was willing to stick by her side. I still am!'

Duncan turned away, then remembered another thing.

'Here's something a bit weird, too. Last weekend was the anniversary of her parent's death. I'll never forget it. January 15th.'

Isaac felt his mouth go dry. 'Eleven years ago?' The words barely came out of his mouth.

'Yeah, eleven years ago. That's why I insisted we have this week in Scotland. Anniversaries are tough. I thought it might help her to be far away from her memories. Ironic, hey?'

'Yes.' But Isaac's thoughts were on something else. Liesel's parents were killed on the same day he married Marylynn! The same day of the same year. There was nothing Isaac could say, and he certainly wasn't going to confide in Duncan about this shared anniversary.

When they finished their coffee, Duncan headed back to the pub.

'Come back tomorrow, and we'll see if we can make some progress,' Isaac offered. He watched him walk down the long driveway, and made sure he was well out of sight, then headed up to Liesel's room. *Their* room.

It occurred to him that although her memory loss had been an accident, maybe part of her didn't want to remember her old life: the grief, the loss, the unacknowledged performance.

Isaac's strong arms were wrapped around her the second he was in the room. 'I've missed you,' he whispered.

'Don't make me go back with him. Promise me. Promise me, Isaac. Tell me I can stay here, with you.'

How could he promise something like that? She belonged to another man's heart. Damn it! No she didn't. Of course he'd fight for her! She was everything to him. Liesel Eather was his whole world.

'I need to go and do some work downstairs for a while. Phone calls to the council about removing the rest of the trees, and so on. I'll come up later.'

Isaac's staff had left their cars down the road and walked up the hill to the castle.

'I love you, Isaac,' she said, her voice soft and fragile.

He kissed her lightly on the forehead, and walked away. Isaac wanted to say he loved her, too, but he knew that it was only going to make it harder when they parted ways. It was best to keep his feelings of love to himself, and so he buried them deep within his heart, building a wall around them. A castle wall. Isaac knew the fortress had to be thick and impenetrable.

It was only a matter of time until he never saw her again. That was the truth, and he had to face up to it. Isaac knew that he needed to come to terms with this intolerable situation now if he was going to survive her leaving him and ending up in the arms of another man.

In his office, he worked solidly for two hours, and then his thoughts were led away. Were they the gentle strains of Schubert's *Serenade* coming through the hallway? At first, he thought he was imagining it. Could it be? Would she have picked up the violin herself? Isaac stole through the ancient hallways of Stoneyhill Castle, almost tiptoeing on the old floorboards so she wouldn't hear him approach. The way she played that instrument was stunning.

The music was exquisite: hauntingly beautiful. It seemed to violate the laws of nature that there wasn't an audience. When she moved on to Debussy's *Clair de Lune*. Isaac felt tears well up, but he didn't bother to brush them away. There was no one there to chastise him or tell him to 'grow up and be a man!' In this rare moment, he could afford himself a little honesty.

And then he heard a scream. Its shrill screeching ripped through the hallways. In a moment of utter violation, he was catapulted from beauty to torture. Isaac rushed into the room, but was too late to stop her. Liesel had wrenched open the window and he watched, helplessly, as she threw the violin out. The crashing sound as it landed on the stone courtyard below, just seconds later, was one of the most violent experiences of his life. What was she thinking?

'Liesel!' He was beside himself. 'Why did you do that?'

She turned to look at him, as if she'd just exorcised a demon.

Isaac ventured closer, wanting to contain her; to protect her from whatever evil thoughts were overwhelming her mind.

'What happens when my memory returns? What if I don't remember you? What...' and she fell into his open, outstretched arms and sobbed. 'What if I never feel love like this again?'

Isaac held her and let her cry while she pounded her fists against his chest.

'If you don't remember what we have, then you'll never know what you're missing,' he said calmly, a lump forming in his parched throat.

'And you?' she asked, looking up with tear-filled eyes.

'I will know…and I'll regret the day I let you walk away!'

'Fight for us! Don't let it happen,' she begged.

'I don't know how to fight for you, Liesel. I'm fighting for someone who craves mangos and wants the sunshine but can't tell me a single thing about who she is. I'm fighting for someone whose heart belongs to another man! I don't know what I have to offer you. I live here as a hermit, because I can't be bothered with the world. I don't want to do that to you. There's a huge world out there, and it needs people like you. When you're not being cranky, you're bright and beautiful, loving, kind, funny. You deserve more than to be stuck here with me.' Isaac shook his head in desperation. 'What am I going to do with you?'

'What do you want to do with me, Isaac?' She shivered beneath his tender touch.

'This…' he whispered, and hungrily lifted her up against him, then carried her to their bed.

Later, he said, 'What do you feel about Duncan?'

'I don't know that man. When I look at him, I can't imagine him touching me the way you do. I don't feel any connection, and it's not just because I can't remember him. I don't feel attraction. I don't feel like I want to kiss him, or slowly take his shirt off. All the things I feel when I look at you...they're real to me. They're all that matters.'

When Duncan arrived ridiculously early at 8am, Isaac ushered him into the kitchen where Liesel was eating porridge. 'Salt? Isaac, salt on porridge? Something doesn't seem right about that.' She shook her head. 'Is this a joke? Maybe I could just have some oat crackers again or a sandwich?'

Isaac laughed. It was as if she was pleading.

'It's not right!' Duncan insisted. 'See, something in your body knows where you've come from: a place which doesn't put salt on porridge. So you must remember other things!' His lack of patience left an unpleasant feeling in the kitchen.

'Duncan, you've got to stop pushing her.'

Isaac broke the news about the violin, edging towards the idea that it was accidental. Furious with her, Duncan fought to keep his rage locked down. His ruddy complexion exploded in a red-hot display of anger. 'How am I supposed to afford another one before the concert tour? That thing—that useless pile of kindling on the ground—was worth $20,000! Your childhood home was sold to buy it.'

'It's meaningless to me.'

'It's bloody irresponsible is what it is. I suppose that since it's insured we might get a payout in time, but I wouldn't know how to replace it or where to buy another one. Only you, that is, the *real* Liesel, would know how to do that.'

Liesel was defiant. 'It wasn't an accident. Duncan, please get out of my life. Whatever it was you think we had, it's over. Stay away.'

Despite Isaac's possessiveness over her, it was wrong for her to drive her fiancé away in this manner. Surely he had to intervene? Wasn't he obligated to give their relationship a fighting chance before he met his own needs?

'Duncan, perhaps you should go home. I'll see to it that she flies back when...'

'No!' She yelled, standing up, her fists clenched. 'No!'

'Liesel, let's just take one day at a time.' Isaac put his hand on her shoulder. What he really wanted to do was take her in his arms and kiss away her pain.

'The specialist is coming tomorrow to examine you. We'll have a better idea...'

'No!' She paced the room like a caged animal, haunted, fearful. Her eyes were wide with terror, as she looked from one man to the other, and back again.

'With all due respect, Mr Heathfield, but I think she sees you as her protector. A father figure.'

'Father figure?' She snapped. 'We're from the same generation!'

There was a palpable shift in the room, and Duncan wondered if she'd fallen for the old hermit. He looked from Isaac to Liesel. Surely not? Not Liesel. Not his Liesel who believed in virginity till marriage, and that relationships were based on friendship first and sex later? He dismissed the thought as crazy.

'She's not going to leave here unless you force her to. She just needs to come back to Australia with me, to see familiar faces and places.' Duncan was quite clear about the path to her recovery.

'No! Isaac, no! Tell him no!' Tears streamed from her eyes.

Isaac took a few deep breaths. Life had never felt so complicated. He'd negotiated million-pound contracts, sometimes in foreign languages, but nothing, nothing was this difficult. He had no tools for handling the complex emotions of human relationships. He never did have. It was simply easier to stay away from other people.

'Duncan, I have a duty of care, and Liesel has a home here for as long as she needs one.'

'You're supposed to be helping us get back together, not tearing us apart!' Duncan was yelling with rage. 'Man, can't you see that she has no incentive to come back as long as she's here? It suits her perfectly to be hidden away and not having to face the world. This is just so bloody like Liesel!'

'I'll call you after the consultant has been, and let you know what he says.' Isaac tried to reassure him.

Was there a part of Liesel that wanted to hide away from the world? He wondered if he wasn't helping her at all, but hindering her progress.

'Shouldn't I be here for that? After all, I'm her next of kin.'

The gravity of those words shook Isaac to the core. Duncan was right. He was the closest person she had to family.

'No!' Liesel walked up to Duncan, and stood just inches away. 'No!'

Isaac allowed Liesel to have the last word. Despite "no" being her favourite word, she came across quite articulately, and he couldn't have said it better himself.

Memories

'Memory can come back slowly, or instantly. Sometimes a sound, a smell or an image can trigger it; other times, it's a shock or surprise. I've no doubt Liesel's memory will return. What I can't tell you is when.' The consultant spoke in hushed tones. 'Cranial trauma can cause retrograde amnesia. It affects episodic memory rather than semantic memory. This is why she can remember words and colours, and everyday things, but not anything specific to her life. Skills are not usually affected.'

'She doesn't appear to remember anything about her life.'

'This type of amnesia usually affects more recent events than remote memories. This is unusual to have the whole slate wiped like this. Sometimes things which happen very close to the time of the accident are never remembered at all, simply because the new memories didn't have strongly embedded neural pathways. I can't give you a cure for this. I'm sorry. Exposing a patient to significant memories or objects from their past can jog their memory, and this will speed up the memory return.'

'What about the concerts in Australia?'

'You say that she seems to have a complete repertoire that she can play. If she was asked to play a particular piece, then it appears she wouldn't be able to do that. Throwing the violin out the window was a good thing, Isaac. Expensive, but good. She's angry at something. It's deep in her subconscious, but it isn't inaccessible. If there's anything you can do to give her a wider experience of the world,' the consultant said, looking around the vast kitchen, 'it would be more likely to prompt a memory than being here in a place which doesn't have any resemblance to the life she knew.'

Isaac reflected on the man's words. 'Thanks for all your help. I appreciate it.'

Then he led the consultant to the front door. His next job was to phone Duncan.

Isaac filled him in on the consultant's thoughts, and then suggested Duncan go back to Australia. 'Put your wedding on hold. It would be wrong for her to marry you. You must agree, surely, that it would be wrong for it to go ahead without her knowing who you are, or, indeed, who she is. In fact, I'm pretty sure it's against the law.'

'Of course it's wrong. I'm just...I don't want to lose her.' Duncan choked at the end of the phone line, and Isaac heard his voice crack under the strain of separation. Isaac felt rotten for him. But... damn it! He didn't want to lose Liesel either.

'I'll make sure she gets there for her concerts. You have my word, but let's take one step at a time. Duncan, for whatever reason, she trusts me. So, I'm asking you to trust me too. I'll get her to the concerts, and I'll make sure she has a concert-standard violin and whatever else she needs.'

'Clothing. She hasn't been shopping yet for her performance clothes. She has terrible taste in clothing. Watch her like a hawk! Concert audiences are not going to expect tie-dye dresses.'

'Leave it to me.'

Isaac was relieved to be off the phone. Of course he'd get Liesel to her concerts, but he sure as hell wasn't leaving her in Australia.

'Pack your passport. That's all you need,' Isaac said, when he kissed her awake the following morning.

'What?'

'I'm taking you on a little trip. Just the two of us. Duncan's gone back to Australia. We're going on a short holiday.'

Liesel looked at him suspiciously. 'This isn't a trick, is it? You're not taking me to Australia? You can't make me go back, you know? You can't force me.'

Isaac felt her shiver, not with cold, but fear.

'No. We're going to Italy. Just you and I. I want to take you to the city of love: Venice. No promises, no expectations; just a short holiday.'

'Why?'

'I thought a change of scenery would be good for us. It's too cold here. Too many staff members around.' Isaac kissed her cheek. 'I want to do this without prying eyes around.' This time he kissed her hungrily, and she responded in kind. 'Trust me. Everything will be perfect.'

'Okay.' She looked him up and down.

Isaac felt so responsible for her: He needed Liesel to trust him, but given that she had no knowledge of her life, of who she was, and of what her future held for her, he had to tread carefully.

A private plane flew them from the local airfield to Edinburgh, then a chartered flight took them on to Venice. A chauffer-driven car met them at the airport, and the driver followed Isaac's instructions. He spoke fluent Italian.

'You speak Italian?' she asked in surprise.

'I'm multi-lingual: Italian, German, Spanish, French and, obviously, English.'

'What use do you have for all these languages when you live an isolated life?'

'I have use for them,' he smiled, and then changed the subject. 'We need to buy you some clothes, and since I've not packed anything for myself, I'll do a spot of shopping too.'

They stepped out onto Calle Vallaresso, and into Dolce and Gabbana. 'Choose anything you want. And remember, you're not backpacking now.' Isaac could have bitten his tongue. Of course she wasn't backpacking. She couldn't even remember her travels around Europe.

Not once did he mention that there was an assortment of postcards in her handbag. They were all written on, ready to post. She'd been to one of the places he planned to take her to on their travels. Isaac hoped it might trigger her memory.

They were a few hours into their shopping spree, and Isaac marvelled that, contrary to Duncan's warning about her clothes choices, she had such good taste, and he silently approved every purchase. Laden with bags, he carried them back to the car where the driver was waiting patiently. Isaac instructed him 'Campo San Moi, 1479. Grazi.'

Prada exuded style and design that was world famous, and Isaac convinced her to purchase many dresses that he thought would be perfect for her concert tour. Several times she commented that she'd have nowhere to wear them.

'You can wear them while we're here, in Italy.

Isaac introduced her to Valentino, at Salizzada San Mois.

'I'm tired of shopping.' She was rather matter of fact about it, but Isaac wasn't entirely sure if such women existed, especially ones who had the option of purchasing everything in sight.

'Can you wait a little bit longer? I need to pick up a few items myself.'

At Ceriello, Isaac selected several Brioni suits, and then before Liesel could argue, they were in Merceria del Capi shopping at Cima. Isaac enjoyed watching her marvel at the luxurious lingerie, and for the first time Isaac noticed her blush. There had been no hint of reservation or shyness when it came to their lovemaking. Quite the opposite. Why was she suddenly so aware of her sexuality? It intrigued him. Was she remembering that she was a virgin prior to their lovemaking? Or could she hear Duncan's angry words in her head? Isaac watched her closely looking for telltale signs of memory returning as her fingers slowly traced the silk ribbons and lace.

'This silk is so smooth,' she sighed. Isaac imagined her wearing the lingerie, and a slight groan rumbled from his lips. Liesel looked up at him and smiled. 'I can't wait to wear it,' she said, and the way she smiled, as if he was the only man in the world, left Isaac weak in the knees. Oh yes, the man of steel was weak for her. Right from the start she'd been kryptonite.

The assistant packed up dozens of pieces of lingerie, and wished them well. 'Can we stop shopping now? I want...'

'I know what you want.' He groaned, and kissed the top of her head. 'I want it too. I want you.'

Although Liesel had no idea whether she'd ever stayed in luxury hotels before, she walked into Gritti Palace Hotel as if she owned it. Perhaps it was the new dress and high-heeled shoes she was wearing, or the way the hairstylist had done her hair a few hours earlier.

Isaac marvelled at how she slipped into her new role. And what was that exactly? He struggled with his conflicting emotions. What plans did he have for her? Realistically, she couldn't stay in Scotland indefinitely. It was no life for someone like Liesel. No, she deserved far more than to be hidden away from the world. And he wanted more for her than that!

The hotel looked across the water to one of Venice's great churches: Santa Maria della Salute. Liesel stood by the window for some time taking in the view, alone in her thoughts. Isaac wrapped his arms around her waist, and looked at the view with her.

'Honey, what are you thinking about? Is there anything you want to talk through?'

'There's so much history here,' she said, absorbing the heritage around her.

'A little bit older than Australia, let's put it that way,' he laughed. 'It dates from 1475.'

Liesel turned and put her arms around his neck. 'Make love to me, Isaac. Right here, right now. I want you, and...I need to know that you want me too.'

Isaac scooped her up in his arms and carried her to the bed.

Everything about his body told Liesel that he wanted her. It was as if his body was a volcano: a wild, explosive force about to erupt. Isaac watched her undress, one item of clothing at a time. He groaned as she exposed her skin.

'Do you want me, Isaac?' she teased, knowing it was all he could do to let her undress herself. Then she began to undress him, kissing his shoulders as she did so. Eventually they were both on the bed, naked and consuming each other; gentle caresses sweeping across their skin. Isaac could feel that she was ready for him, and couldn't comprehend how someone who'd had so little sexual experience could guide him into her body so expertly. Liesel's confidence aroused him even more. Isaac sank deep into her recess, comforting himself in the alcove of pleasure. Nectar seeped around them both, and together they rocked back and forward. Lovemaking was slow, deliberate and tender. He found a rhythm which sated them, but he was still hungry: so hungry to have her, that his actions became urgent; unrestrained, and desperately seeking her in the only way he knew how.

Liesel's body wasn't her own. It turned Isaac on even more to know that it was him, and him alone, who was having this catastrophic effect on her senses. He'd never seen her respond like this. What demons was he exorcising from her body? Torrents of violent delight: a contradiction of sensations, rippled through them. One final thrust and they were both flying over the edge. Pulsations echoing in every cell. Isaac moaned as he sank his head between the pillows of her breasts. Sated. Satisfaction achieved. Isaac Heathfield never wanted this moment to end. And then his heart ripped in half: surely it was like caging a beautiful bird to keep her tucked away in the Highlands?

'I'm going to love you forever,' she whispered.

Some time later, he invited her to shower with him. Against the tiles, he held her. Pinning her firmly with his hands, his lips were kind, soft, inviting. Luring her towards the prize, he felt her melting beneath him. Was it possible to want her again, so soon? His body pounded between them. Barely able to stand, he moved closer so she could feel his arousal. A moan of delight, at the promises which awaited, escaped her lips.

'What are you waiting for?' she teased, breathlessly.

Isaac lifted her lithe legs up around him, and held her securely. Internal humidity rendered him powerless. Once again, he was under her spell. Adroit, he made his way home: physically powerful, masterful, exquisitely strong; knocking at the ceiling of her cave until she answered, until she called out, until she had no choice but to tear the walls down and tell the world she'd surrendered! That she was his, and his alone.

Slowly, ever so slowly, coming down from their high, they held each other as the steamy water cascaded over them. Collapsing onto the floor, their hands touched each other's faces, exploring, laughing, loving, learning. Every day they were discovering secrets about each other. Every day their lives were becoming more firmly enmeshed. Isaac Heathfield was the only memory she needed. Or, at least, he hoped that he was the only one she needed.

Isaac escorted her to dinner in The Gritti's *Club de Doge* restaurant.

'This dining room is exquisite,' she whispered.

'One of the best in the world, my darling.'

Isaac loved that her cheeks were still flushed from lovemaking, a visible reminder of their passion; he wanted to advertise to the whole world that the beautiful woman he was with had just been in his arms; in his bed.

'Am I? Am I your darling, Isaac?' she asked uncertainly.

'Of course you are. Haven't I just spent the past hours showing you that?'

'Then don't forget it. And don't let me go.'

Isaac couldn't bear the uncertainty in her eyes, any more than the fear and confusion which pooled up at the edges.

Afterwards, he treated her to the Acqua di Parma spa. Even if she didn't know it, she deserved pampering; and Isaac wanted to ease every last cellular memory of pain out of her body.

The hotel was intimate, and the staff charming. They drank Dama Bianca coffee at the bar, gently stroking each other's hands as they were serenaded by the soulful strings of a mandolin. Finally, they returned to their room.

Their suite overlooked the Grand Canal.

'I have lots of plans for us tomorrow. But tonight, my love, we sleep.'

And they fell into each other's arms, as if they'd always been there. As if it was the most comfortable place in the world: the only place.

After a long leisurely breakfast, they travelled the waterways taking in the historical sights of the city of love. There were serenaded in the weak morning sunshine of late Winter.

'This is the Museo della Musica,' he said.

The music museum was housed in Chiesa di San Maurizio, a restored, neoclassical building.

'Why are you bringing me here, Isaac? I don't want to see violins.'

He laughed inside at the irony. There had been seven postcards of this place in her handbag, and each one had her writing passionately on the other side of it. All those memories were buried deep inside her and he was at a loss to how she could retrieve them.

'This is a collection of rare and curious 17th to 19th century instruments. I thought it would be interesting,' he said patiently, wondering if she'd remember the postcard she'd written to Duncan about how incredible it all was.

'Isaac, don't do this.'

'Don't fight me, Liesel. I'm on your side, damn it! Never forget that. Every single second, I am on *your* side. I'm fighting for you, not against you.' His words were firm: 'I'm fighting for both of us; for our lives. Let me do this!'

He watched and leaned in as she searched his eyes, trying to anchor herself there, and remained silent. And he could see that she knew he was right; that he was on her side and was fighting for them both.

They toured the museum holding hands. Isaac held her in his arms for some time, and touched her for most of the afternoon. Words were pointless. She needed to know that he was there for her, and he let his body do the talking, stopping from time to time to kiss her, and hold her tight.

Isaac promised Liesel a wonderful night out in Venice, and by early evening, they were at San Vidal. It was a popular concert venue, renowned for Vivaldi's music being performed on historical instruments. Isaac braced himself for her reaction.

Liesel sighed when she saw the poster: *Violini a Venezia*. 'I don't speak Italian, Isaac, but it looks to me like we're seeing a violin concert! What are you trying to do to me?'

'*Interpreti Venziani* is a brilliant string orchestra. We can't possibly come to Venice and not watch them play,' he explained, hoping she'd catch onto his enthusiasm.

As Isaac held her hand throughout the evening, he couldn't help notice her enjoying the orchestra; her foot was tapping, and her breathing accelerated during various pieces. Something was happening inside, he just wasn't sure what. And he doubted she knew what was happening, either.

The next few days were spent exploring Venice, dining in style, and enjoying the city. The Winter was much milder here than in the Highlands, and felt like a pleasant retreat from the ice-cold days they'd shared.

In the evenings, they retreated to their room, safe in each other's arms. Every day they spent together was like a lifetime. Isaac made it his mission to create a world of memories for Liesel: beautiful, life-altering, pleasurable memories.

He was fighting for her memory, for their memory. Fighting for their love, and their future.

The following day, they stopped in front of an old building with security guards by the front door.

'What is this place?' she asked, unable to read the language.

'It's an auction house.'

'What are we doing here?'

Isaac smiled. 'Shopping.'

For a few seconds, he almost thought he saw a twinkle in her eyes, a sense of recognition, perhaps, when she saw a table with violins laid out at the front of the room. There were security guards, and some violins were in bolted glass chambers.

Isaac guided her to a seat and said 'Make yourself comfortable. I'll be back in a moment.'

Isaac went and picked up a brochure of the violins for auction, and then returned to her.

'I know this won't mean anything to you, but let me read through it anyway. Humour me.'

'I don't want to buy a violin, Isaac, and I certainly don't have the sort of money that these probably cost. In fact, I believe you told me there was only £200 in my purse.'

'I'm buying it. And I want you to let me do that for you. It's your birthday next week. This is my gift to you. It's part of your recovery. I can't choose it for you because I don't know what I'm looking for.'

'And you think I do?' she muttered in hushed tones.

'Just feel it. Listen to the sound. That's all you need to do. You'll know what's right for you. The auction doesn't start for another hour. You've got time to look at each one, so take your time. There's no pressure.'

'Everything about this is pressure. You promised that I don't have to do the concerts, so why should I get a violin?'

'You have a gift, Liesel. A gift.'

'A gift I don't remember! You can't make me do those concerts.'

'I'm not going to make you. But…what if I came with you? What if I was by your side for each concert? What if I stayed with you the whole time?' His eyes never left hers. Isaac held her with his promise; an oath of commitment and security.

'You'd do that?'

'Of course I would! Just five concerts. Look, count them on your fingers. You can do this. One concert at a time. I'll be right there on left stage by your side. Watching you, clapping for you. I'll be there. I won't let you out of my sight. I promise.'

She didn't agree, but for the first time she didn't

argue with him either.

'I'm scared.'

'I know you are.' Isaac held her hand reassuringly. 'Will you look at the violins? For me?'

'For you?'

'Yes, for me. Do it for *me*.' Isaac knew it was wrong, but he had to play to her weak spot. Isaac was the centre of her universe, and he used that to help her move forward: to take the next big step.

'Yes.'

Isaac smiled, then read through the literature. 'This is a Guarneri. Does that mean anything to you?'

Liesel raised her eyebrows and shoulders helplessly as if to say 'what do you think?'

'The Guarneri family was from Cremona in Northern Italy during the 17th century. Three generations of that family produced some of the finest violins the world has ever known,' he said, and continued to read through the information: *Giuseppe's violins were different to the other violin makers in his family, and had a unique style and sound.*

'May I?' she tentatively asked the security guard.

The man unlocked the glass box, and passed the instrument to her.

Liesel looked it up and down, then into Isaac's eyes.

'You can do it,' he whispered.

When the first strains glided off the strings, a hushed silence filled the space. Conversations stopped. People drew closer. No one recognised the young violinist, but they acknowledged the sounds of someone who'd toiled for thousands upon thousands of hours. Isaac wiped a tear from his eye.

Liesel truly had no idea of her talent.

'What does it feel like?' he asked.

'Nice, I guess. I can't tell you. I'm not aware of even playing it, really. I can't describe it.'

'Don't worry. Try some more instruments. You'll know when you've found the right one.'

Liesel tried more than a dozen violins, each time feeling somewhat exasperated. 'Can I try the Guarneri again?'

'Of course.' Isaac spoke in Italian to the security guard.

The man passed her the instrument.

Liesel looked into Isaac's eyes, desperate for a sign. Was this the right instrument? She lifted the bow, with no idea of what she'd play or how she'd play. Paganini's *La Campagnella* filled the room.

Spontaneous applause erupted!

Liesel looked around her. They were clapping for her and the music she was making. She was stunned.

A man came over and spoke in swift Italian, wanting to organise concerts. *Who was she?*, he wanted to know. Isaac translated for her. 'That piece is one of the most difficult to play on the violin. He says you played it as if it's the easiest.'

When Isaac choked back a tear, Liesel said 'I'll have this violin.'

At once elated and feeling guilty, Isaac knew that all she wanted was to make him happy. The auction went well into the afternoon, and the Guarneri was the last item to be presented.

Liesel's eyes watered as Isaac fought with a German buyer and the price went to double the auctioneer's starting price.

'Isaac, I don't need the violin. I only want it to keep you happy. Don't pay that sort of money, please.'

'Sold! Sold to Mr Heathfield of Scotland,' boomed the auctioneer's voice in hesitant English.

'I can't believe you just did that.' Liesel squeezed his hand. 'You did that for me.'

'Honey, promise me one thing,' he pleaded.

'Yes, anything. Anything at all. I'll do anything for you.'

Isaac sensed her desperation.

'Don't throw it out the window.'

'I promise.'

Discovery

When they returned to Stoneyhill Castle, Isaac encouraged Liesel to spend some time getting to know the violin and explained about the neurons in the brain, and how she was developing new memories all the time. Even though she instinctively knew how to play the instrument, it was well worth her time continuing to play and giving new messages to her brain. Every day, for several hours, she'd stand in the large kitchen playing a variety of pieces. Isaac was nearby in his office, listening the whole time while he worked. Today he wondered why she kept playing Pachelbel's *Canon* over and over. It must be the eleventh time now. Was she trying to perfect it? Maybe she was remembering something. Isaac wasn't sure whether to interrupt Liesel or leave her to play on her own. And then the music stopped. Isaac panicked. The thought of that instrument striking the ground rendered his legs like jelly. Standing up, and making sure he had use of his legs, he gathered his thoughts together and prepared to find her.

'Can I come in?' Liesel asked, standing at the door to his office. Although she had seen him enter the room earlier, she hadn't been in the room at any time during her stay. Liesel looked around it curiously.

'Of course, come and take a seat.' Isaac stood up and met her half way across the room. Liesel moved into his arms, as if in a state of relief. Isaac's breathing had calmed down, and he was grateful that the violin was still in one piece.

'Are you okay?' he asked, kissing her softly on the top of her head.

'I don't know. There was a piece I was playing, and...'

'You remember something?'

'No, but it feels like I do. It's like it's touching something inside me but I can only feel it. I can't see it or hear it.'

'That's okay. Remember, one day at a time.'

'What is this room?' she asked, taking in the floor-to-ceiling bookshelves.

'My office.'

'Office? Do castle owners have jobs?' she asked, not quite sure if it was a stupid question. 'You *work*?'

'Some of us do,' he laughed.

Isaac studied her as she wandered around the room, gently touching different items: a globe, his fountain pen, and a photo of a man who looked like it could have been his father.

'Who is this?' she asked.

'My father.'

'Where does he live?'

'He died.'

'I'm so sorry. Isaac, I'm sorry.'

'No need to be.'

'What happened?'

Such a simple question, such a complicated answer!

Isaac walked to the huge window overlooking the loch. 'He inherited this castle from his father, and just about all the land you can see for miles around. Castles need to be run like businesses, and he let it get into a state of disrepair. The surrounding farms needed regular maintenance, and he just didn't keep on top of things. Day by day his debts increased until things became insurmountable. My father drank every day.'

Isaac was silent for a few moments. 'He took his own life.'

Liesel held her hand to her chest.

'One freezing Winter's day, he walked into the loch. No goodbye, no explanation!' Isaac kicked the floor.

Liesel raced to put her arms around him, and sobbed.

'I'm so sorry.'

Isaac held her close, appreciating her deep-level care. It was impossible not to think of his father whenever he looked at the loch; and the icy waters which claimed his life.

'Although I was the heir to all this, I'd never really lived here. I grew up in boarding school from the age of five. My mother was heartbroken at being separated from me, and ran off to America by the time I was six. I haven't seen her since.'

Isaac wished she hadn't asked these questions. It was obvious that she was highly empathic, and that his past was too painful to comprehend.

'She didn't keep in touch with you? She...she *abandoned* you?'

'That's what it felt like.'

'That's what it *was* like! How could a mother do such a thing?'

'I think it was the beginning of the end for my father when she left. Instead of me coming home for holidays, he'd ship me off to my aunties and friends. We rarely saw each other.'

'If he was in debt, and you weren't raised here, then how did you know what to do? Are there classes in being a castle owner?' She was deadly serious, and the way she asked made Isaac laugh out loud.

'No! There are no classes in that sort of thing.'

'What did you do?'

'I relied on other skills. I took out a crippling mortgage from the bank. From several banks!'

'But what do you do to bring in money? What do you sell?'

Isaac didn't answer her, but kissed her on the forehead and returned to his desk.

'Nothing you need to be concerned with.'

And with a growing sense of unease, he watched as she wandered to the bookshelves.

'You like reading?'

'Yes, I do.' What he really wanted to say was: stay away from the books, and leave me alone.

'You haven't read much since I've been here then? I haven't seen you reading.'

'No, I haven't.'

Liesel perused the shelves, and then came to one with dozens of books by the same writer.

'Who is this author? Heath Zackary? You've got a *lot* of his books. Is he a big name then?'

'You could say that.' Isaac smiled as she looked through all the titles. 'So, your lack of memory hasn't affected your ability to read?'

Liesel looked at him as if it was an odd question. 'What genre are they?'

'Mystery. Paranormal. Romance,' he smiled.

'You read *romance* novels?'

The look of shock on her face made him smile. 'Romance?' she continued. 'You?'

Isaac chuckled. 'Doesn't everyone need a little love in their lives?'

'I suppose, but...*you?*'

Liesel shook her head, not quite able to comprehend the man she'd come to know reading love stories.

'You don't think I'm romantic, then, Ms Eather? Candlelight dinners, holiday in Venice, lovemaking in the moonlight. These aren't romantic gestures?'

'Well, you did beautifully arrange the bathroom and create a relaxed ambience, and you always light a candle when we eat. And you filled our hotel room with fresh flowers and chocolates. Why do you have his books in other languages? Is it to help you with your multilingual skills? Is that how you learnt to speak those languages?'

'So many questions, Liesel,' he laughed, trying to shrug off her curiosity. 'We should have some coffee. Let's go to the kitchen,' he said, hoping to distract her.

If they stayed here any longer, he was going to have to tell her. Liesel was asking way too many questions. For years, he'd kept it a secret. *Years!* No one but his agent knew who Heath Zackary really was. And possibly Adalene, but they'd never discussed it; she simply dusted the shelves each Monday morning.

Liesel turned abruptly, as if she'd had a revelation. When their eyes met, lightning struck.

'You're a writer.'

Isaac noted that she didn't ask it as a question; she didn't query it. There was no need. Isaac could tell that she knew.

'You've written all these books. This is how you earn your living.'

'Yes.' And for a fleeting moment he wondered if she'd lose interest in him now that he wasn't some wealthy castle owner. Now that he was just a writer.

'Wow. That's incredible! I can't wait to read them. This is amazing. Which one should I start with?'

'You want to read them?' He was incredulous. Isaac lived his creative life firmly in the closet. The isolated world of the Highlands suited his muse perfectly. But now his secret was ousted by the best thing that had ever happened to him.

'May I?' she asked, scooping an armful of books off the shelf without waiting for an answer.

'Take a seat. Make yourself at home. I've got a chapter to finish, but perhaps we could have something to eat after that?' But he'd already lost her. Within seconds she was deep into the first page of *The Stone Child*.

Isaac didn't get back to his writing but spent the next few hours watching her. Every facial expression had him intrigued, and he knew exactly where she was at any point in the story by the way her face mirrored his words. This was the first time he'd ever seen anyone read his books: his international, best-selling novels; and it was a revelation to him watching someone so engrossed in every word. Isaac knew what was coming next, though, by the way she was laughing. And then he pulled some tissues from the box and walked over to her. Liesel wouldn't be laughing for long.

Then she reached for the tissues, sobbing like a distraught child.

'Honey, it's not real. I'm glad you're taken by the story, but remember, it's just an invention of my imagination.'

'You're wrong. It's real. It's the story of every little child who has ever lost a parent. It's *your* story.'

And yours, he thought to himself. *And yours*. While she may not consciously remember her parents' passing, her body did.

Isaac held her while she cried. It hadn't occurred to him that his books might prove to be quite therapeutic for her.

'When you've finished that book, read *Pretty Prison*.'

Isaac caught the suspicion in her eyes.

'Just read it,' he urged.

That night, he regretted that she'd found his library of self-penned works. They'd probably never make love again, not when there were so many stories to read: tears to cry, smiles to turn to laughter, and deep longing sighs. 'Just one more sentence,' she'd whisper, and then 'Just one more page.'

'Are you coming to bed, Liesel?'

'Just one more chapter. Ssshhh.'

That was it, he'd lost her. He reckoned he should be grateful, though, that she loved to read.

Liesel spent almost every waking moment with her face inside one of his novels. 'Why do you hide away? Why don't you want to be famous? Why can't the world know who you really are?'

'Perhaps it's a fall-out from a childhood spent in boarding school. From as far back as I can remember, I had to share a room with twenty other boys. There was never any privacy or time to oneself. I was a deep thinker with a rich imagination, and boarding school tried to knock that out of me. I excelled at English, and my father was despondent that I didn't go on to be something great, like a judge. "A writer?" he asked one day. "No son, you can't do that." So, I led him to believe I was heading into business studies so that I had something solid behind me for when I eventually inherited the castle. The truth is that I'd be quite happy living in a one-room hut.'

'Why don't you then?'

'I've come to love the sense of history with this place, and I've done a lot of work to restore it. I feel it is my duty to preserve this place for future generations. There's nothing quite as disheartening as a strong ancient building falling into ruin. It's been in my family since the beginning. I feel a sense of responsibility to keep it in this family, even if I never have children. Even if...the family line stops with me.'

'Do you want children?'

'Yes.'

'Do you want to have children with me, Isaac?'

'Liesel, don't... don't go there. Right now, we've got too many obstacles in our way to even contemplate such a possibility.'

'If we didn't have those obstacles, then would you...'

'Liesel, don't...'

There was no chance of giving her a straight answer while their future was so up in the air.

'Do you ever wonder about opening this place up to other people in some way?'

'I have the occasional summer party,' he smiled. 'For close friends.'

'You could offer boutique five-star accommodation at certain times of the year...or...'

'Or what?'

'Nothing. It was a silly idea.'

'Tell me.'

'Concerts outside in the park...on Summer evenings.'

Isaac's eyes lit up. 'That sounds like a wonderful idea.' He was intrigued by her business mind. 'Would you help to organise something like that?'

'Really? Would you want me to?'
'I'd love it!'

Under the Spotlight

Adalene helped Liesel pack for her trip to Australia. It was primarily made up of items from her Italian shopping spree.

'Have a lovely time my dear. I'm sure you'll be absolutely wonderful. You'll have audiences in tears.'

'Thank you, Adalene.' Liesel felt a little nervous. What lay ahead? Who would she meet? What would she remember? Terrified of having to spend time with Duncan, she kept saying to Isaac that seeing him again was the last thing she wanted. Why couldn't she remember him? Why did she feel so uncomfortable around him? So disconnected; and as if he made her skin crawl?

Isaac surprised Liesel with a few days in Bali. Desperate to do anything to preserve their relationship, he sought ways to lengthen the amount of time they spent alone together.

'Happy birthday, my darling!' he said when she woke up that morning in their beach-side villa.

They'd arrived late at night, after their long-haul flight. This morning she stood in a charming villa, by the open window, taking in spacious ocean views and splendid mountain ranges. A short while later, a knock on the door brought them a fine breakfast prepared by an Indonesian chef.

Liesel was treated to a facial, manicure, pedicure, massage and they enjoyed a stroll along the beach. Their clandestine setting meant they could make love on the shores with complete privacy.

Isaac introduced her to his favourite Balinese towns and foods.

'How many times have you been here?' she asked, surprised at how he seemed to know where everything was, and shocked that some people knew his name.

'I come here a couple of times a year. Mostly for the sunshine! It's my antidote to the long Scottish Winters. It helps with my research though, particularly if I've got Indonesian-based settings or characters. Google might be a source of infinite information, but nothing a writer pens will ever match their experience of a place.'

They wandered by batik makers' stalls, and jewellery stands.

Isaac smiled at how Liesel caught her breath at some of the stone-carved temples, and how she chatted for hours with a museum curator about pieces of art.

Isaac noted that she had a natural flare for choosing indigenous art which spoke of love.

Afterwards they sipped coffee in a street café.

'Can we live here?' she asked breathlessly. 'I never want to leave these crystal-clear waters and sandy beaches. The skies are the most beautiful blue. And the sunlight is incredible. Unless you can take the Sun back to Scotland, then let's just live here.'

Isaac knew he'd give her the Moon, if he could, or the Sun, but right now his priority was for her to remember. He watched her feast on passionfruits, ripping the tough purple skins with her teeth. That she did it so naturally made him smile. *She remembers.* She remembers how to eat passionfruit. They sipped young coconut juice under the palm trees, and later that day he taught her how to shop for Indonesian spices.

On their last night in Bali, they sat on the shoreline, their bare feet dipped into the fine sand. The Sun was red, and sank seamlessly into the horizon. It reflected on the water, the beauty of which brought tears to her eyes.

'I don't want to leave, Isaac. Why can't we stay?'

'Apart from the little issue of visas? We have to go to Australia, Liesel. You have commitments there.'

She sighed. 'Thank you for all of the memory making. I hope I never forget these days with you.'

'Me neither.' Isaac held her close, his arms around her as she nestled into the embrace of his whole body. 'Me neither.'

'For Australian citizens returning to Australia, welcome home,' the air stewardess's voice was amplified across the plane as they touched the runway at Sydney International Airport.

'I don't feel like I'm coming home,' she whispered nervously.

'One baby step at a time. Nothing more, nothing less. Duncan's going to meet us a few hours before you're due to play at the Sydney Opera House tomorrow night. Let's go and freshen up at the hotel, and take a nap.'

As they wandered into the Shangri-la Hotel, Isaac said 'This is the finest accommodation in the southern hemisphere. It will be our sanctuary for the next few days. You'll be safe here.'

Once they were in their suite, they stood hand in hand taking in the stunning panoramic views. 'Do you recognise the harbour bridge or the opera house?'

Liesel looked at him like he was an idiot.

'Of course I do.'

'Do you remember performing there when you were fifteen?'

She didn't answer. If she couldn't remember playing there, then she probably didn't remember that fateful day when her parents died. Now was not the time to cause her sadness.

The following afternoon, Isaac called the concierge to bring Liesel's violin from the hotel's safe.

After holding it in her hands for a while, she positioned herself and played a piece. 'The tuning sounds alright, I guess. Why do I feel so unprepared? Do I need to practise some more?'

Isaac smiled. 'No, you don't need to. Your body is sensing something huge. It's triggering the subconscious. Just because you don't consciously remember, it doesn't mean that your body doesn't hold a memory of what it's like to perform.'

'What if I run out of pieces to play, or play the same piece twice?'

'You'll be fine, absolutely fine. I promise you, there is nothing for you to worry about.'

That evening, Isaac helped her dress, doing up the tiny buttons on her exquisite royal-purple gown. 'You look amazing. Truly amazing. Beautiful. I knew this dress was a perfect choice.'

Isaac wanted to get her to the opera house early, just in case Duncan tried to see them beforehand. The last thing that Isaac wanted was Duncan discovering that they were sharing a bed. The deception was devastatingly uncomfortable, but he didn't feel he had much choice right now. There was no telling what choices Liesel would make when her memory came back. *If* it came back.

Once they were at the opera house, they were escorted to Liesel's dressing room. Isaac was surprised by her lack of nerves. Perhaps that was a good thing. The room was reserved for top talent, and already it was filled with bouquets from well-wishers. Bowls of exotic fruits and glossy high-quality magazines were set onto the marble and gold tables. The hairdresser and make-up artist tended to her, and transformed her look into that of a world-class entertainer. Their chat was light and friendly, and Isaac admired the way that Liesel just relaxed into the situation.

Her agent, Julia, was the first person to visit, and then her music teacher, Janelle. They buoyed her up, and despite how nervous they felt at her complete lack of memory, they also trusted her enough to know that she could carry this off. Neither of them felt entirely comfortable working with her when she had no memory of them. But they were thankful that Isaac was there as a bridge between both worlds: past and present.

Julia said that she was already inundated by calls from people who wanted to organise more concerts, and that she couldn't begin to imagine what it would be like after Liesel actually performed.

'She can't commit to anything at this point,' Isaac warned. 'Perhaps when her memory returns we can have this conversation? For now, it's just not something she can enter into.'

Julia agreed that that was the best plan of action. Janelle listened to Liesel play a few pieces, and was more than happy with her tone and technique. There was no reason to fear the night ahead. They headed off to take a seat in the audience, excited about seeing 'their' virtuoso take to the stage for her debut performance as an adult.

Duncan arrived, and nearly choked on his tongue to see how exquisite Liesel looked in her gown and the hair and make-up transformation. She'd emerged from the casual girl he'd known for years to an elegant and sophisticated lady. 'You...are...beautiful! I've never seen you look so stunning. Leez, you're incredible!'

She blushed, and looked over to Isaac claiming his gaze as if her life depended on it. They were words she only wanted to hear from him, not this strange man standing before her.

'So babe, are you all set?'

'Don't call me...'

'I'm sorry!' He hit his fist against the wall in frustration. 'You never minded before.'

'I'm not that person.'

'Five minutes till curtain up, Ms Eather,' a young runner said, popping her head around the door. 'Five minutes.'

'Okay, Liesel. Remember, I'll be left of the stage. I'll be there the whole time. I won't be going anywhere.'

'I'll be there too,' Duncan chimed in.

Liesel gave him a look which said in no uncertain terms: *no you will not.*

'Damn it, Liesel! You're meant to be my wife by now!'

'Duncan, this isn't the time. Tonight isn't about you. This is Liesel's night. If she doesn't want you there, you owe it to her to respect that.' Isaac was firm, but kind.

'I'll see you after the show,' he muttered, shaking his head in exasperation.

Isaac's heart pounded inside his chest. What if she stumbled? What if she looked into the crowd and panicked? *What if...*

But there were no what-ifs. Liesel played like a dream.

Standing ovations entwined with roars from the crowd and hushed silences. Liesel's repertoire was rich and varied. Even though she had no idea from piece to piece what she was going to play or what they were called or how long they went for, each time she simply lifted the violin to her chin, and raised the bow. Music flowed like wine, satisfying the palate of everyone in the audience. Although she had no idea of the order the music would be played, her repertoire included:

The Dance Of The Goblins, by Bazzini
Moto Perpetuo, by Paganini
The Flight Of The Bumblebee, by Rimsky-Korsakov
Serenade Melancolique, by Tchaikovsky

The finale was a breathtaking performance of Ravel's *Tzigane*.

'I did it,' she whispered to Isaac when she finally left the stage, covering her ears from the roar of the crowd. 'I did it.'

'Yes, my darling, you most certainly did.' Isaac embraced Liesel, and was about to kiss her when he caught Duncan's eye. 'She was great, wasn't she?' he said as Duncan approached; and carefully, but reluctantly, let her go.

'Brilliant, babe. Brilliant.'

'Don't call her babe, Duncan. She doesn't like it.'

Feeling somewhat chastised, Duncan changed the subject.

'I want to take you home, Liesel. Let's go back to your house. Your flatmate Jess is missing you like crazy. If you go back, it might help you to remember. You know, seeing your bedroom, your clothes, your cat....'

'I have a cat?'

'Mozart. He's called Mozart.'

'Sweet,' she laughed.

Liesel looked up at Isaac. She couldn't read him. What was he thinking? An inch of panic spasmed in the depths of her belly. It was all she could do not to wrap her arms around him. Isaac was her anchor in uncertain waters and she relied on him to keep her strong, safe, secure.

What he was thinking was that he didn't want her to remember her old life, or that she was meant to be with Duncan. If she could read his mind she'd know that he wanted to take her back to the hotel, make love to her all night long, and finish the other four concerts and take her back home. Home to Scotland. But he couldn't say that to her, and certainly not to Duncan.

'Perhaps we can drop by in a few days, after the Melbourne and Adelaide concerts,' Isaac suggested. 'It's far too late to go there now.'

'Drop by? This is her home. She lives a few miles from here. She shouldn't be dropping by! Liesel should be going home.'

Isaac didn't argue, but simply said 'She's going to do her other concerts first.'

Duncan's fury was palpable. 'Who the hell gives you the authority to take over Liesel's life like this?'

The next two concerts added to Liesel's confidence, and she now played the violin during the day as well.

Isaac noted that she seemed to really be enjoying her rehearsals. After her concert in Adelaide, he decided to treat her to the sights of the city by hiring a tandem bicycle. They cycled through parklands, and city streets. Stopping for ice cream in the park, Isaac asked if she was happy.

'Yes, I'm so happy. I'm happy when I am with you. That's all I need.'

Later, they headed up to the Adelaide Hills, wandering the tree-lined streets of Stirling, and sipped coffee in a café.

Isaac had enjoyed being away from Duncan's prying eyes, and the other people who knew Liesel well. He'd needed this time away, too. Time to just be with her. Uncertain about when or whether her memory would return, or if she'd even want to be with him, all he could do was live one day at a time, and trust, pray and hope with all his heart that she was right: they were destined to be together. It was a long shot, a dream, a fairytale, and it made him even more determined to claim ownership over every second they shared.

Reluctantly, they headed back to Sydney, and caught a taxi to Liesel's home that she shared with Jessica. Liesel stood at the front gate, wondering if she had any memories of this place.

It was a wooden bungalow, set into a quarter-acre garden. The large verandah wrapped around three sides of the red-roofed house.

Mature trees and shrubs were dotted around the garden, and the scented path was lined with rosemary, lavender and apple berry. She brushed her hands along the herbs, and breathed in the scent. Nothing. Not a single memory about her home.

'I feel so nervous about meeting her. Duncan says

we're best friends, but her name doesn't mean anything to me.'

'Everything will come back to you in its own time. Your body had a severe trauma, Liesel. You can't push your recovery.' He held her hand, and then kissed her forehead.

They knocked on the door of Liesel's home, and were met at the door by a vibrant young woman, with short blonde hair, of a similar age.

'Leez! You're home! You're finally home!' Jess screamed with delight. She reached over and hugged Liesel, and was dismayed that the feeling of joy wasn't reciprocated.

'I'm sorry,' Liesel said. 'I just don't remember you. Or anything.'

Jess looked helplessly at Isaac.

'Come inside. I'll make us a drink,' she said, inviting them into the wooden bungalow.

'I couldn't get tickets to your concert. It was sold out. I was so gutted. Dunc says you were brilliant!'

'She was great,' Isaac said.

The cat purred contentedly when Liesel picked him up. 'Mozart, hey? I'm sorry little man, but I don't remember you. I sure would like to though. You're mighty cute.'

Jessica laughed. 'The day you found him stranded on the sidewalk you acted like it was the happiest day of your life. You were ripe for mothering this little fella. Sure is good to have you home again, Leez. Where are your things?'

'I'm not staying, Jessica. I...I can't move back in here when I don't even remember anything.'

Jessica's face fell. 'But...'

'I'll cover the rent, and any associated costs,' Isaac

said gently. 'It's probably best if Liesel's things go into storage, and then you can get another flatmate if you like. I'll arrange to get things moved.'

'But,' Jessica wanted to protest. She had no reason to distrust or dislike Isaac, but she just wasn't comfortable with her best friend living this other life.

'At least go into your bedroom. Take a look around,' she urged her friend.

Liesel put the cat down, and looked at Isaac. 'Will you come with me?'

'Of course.'

Jessica pointed the way, and left them to it.

'I feel like I'm going through a stranger's things. It feels wrong.'

'I can only begin to imagine,' he said softly, looking at a photo of Liesel and Duncan all loved-up on the beach. His heart sank. Isaac's joy was another man's suffering. Isaac picked up the photo and passed it to her.

'I don't know him. I don't feel anything when I look at that, except…I really needed a haircut, and my bikini was the wrong colour.'

Isaac laughed.

'What about this?' he asked, picking up a photo of what must have been her parents.

'I don't know who they are.'

'You don't recognise them at all?'

'No, should I?'

'They're your parents, Liesel.'

'Should we visit them? I guess they'll be worried.'

Curse! He couldn't tell her. Not now. Not here. Later, when they were somewhere more private.

'Look through your wardrobe,' he said, changing the subject. 'See if there's anything you want.'

When she opened the doors and pulled out jeans, blouses, skirts and shoes, she exclaimed 'These are horrible. They can't be mine. These can *not* be mine!'

'Well, they're interesting choices,' he smiled, taking in her eclectic bohemian wardrobe.

'I want to go home, Isaac. The concerts were fun, but do I have to do any more? Can't we just go home, or...'

'Or what?'

'Or go back to Bali?'

'I promise with all my heart that we'll go back there when we sort out a visa for you. You have my word.'

Isaac ignored Duncan's call coming through on the mobile phone. If he could, he'd just squish him out of existence like an annoying insect. He hated himself for such callous feelings, but as each day passed it became more unbearable to think of life without Liesel at his side.

'Who's that?' she asked, watching the anger on Isaac's face.

'Duncan.' He tried to say it calmly, but didn't succeed.

'Agggh. I wish he'd just go away! I find him incredibly annoying. I would never, *ever*, date someone like that.'

'How do you know? Really, Liesel? You don't remember anything. How do you know what you like or don't like? You don't.'

'How I feel right now is that I'm not remotely drawn to him. With or without my memory, I trust my gut feelings on this. He's not my type.'

Isaac called Jessica, and arranged to get some boxes; then he spent the afternoon packing up Liesel's possessions. The smaller boxes he arranged to have sent straight to Stoneyhill Castle. The furniture could go to charity. He laughed at her basic, el cheapo underwear. So she used to be a no-frills girl, he chuckled to himself. *No wonder she blushed in Italy. Some part of her knew.*

Jess had a thing or two to say about moving Liesel's possessions out. 'It's a bit presumptuous, Isaac. Once her memory is back, she won't want to be in Scotland. She hates the cold. She only went there because Duncan insisted there was some place he wanted to see there: a haunted loch or something.'

Isaac winced. There was a certain irony that it was Duncan who encouraged Liesel to visit the loch, and to glimpse the castle.

'Her whole life is here. Her friends, her music, her fiancé...' she continued.

'Is that enough? Was she happy? Was she fulfilled?'

'You think she's in love with you, don't you?' Jessica asked, shocked that reliable, old-fashioned, high-morals-at-every-turn Liesel would actually be with another man.

'The feeling is mutual, I can assure you.'

'Does Duncan know?' she gasped in horror.

'Not yet, and I'd appreciate it if he didn't find out. Liesel will need to tell him herself, and it really is best to come from her but only when the time is right. When her memory has returned.'

'Do you think she'll stay with you when she remembers what she had? What she'd be giving up?'

'I can't honestly answer that. I just pray she values her present as much as her past.'

'I hope you have a strong heart, Isaac. You're playing with fire here. Liesel is one feisty girl. Duncan always thought she was laid-back, a pushover, but that's not who she was at all. He really didn't know her as well as he thought he did. She's as strong as they come, and once she makes up her mind about something, then there's no stopping her.'

'Well *that* part hasn't changed!'

'Her clothing choices have though. Really odd!'

Isaac smiled. 'Something positive, then?'

They laughed, and found a quiet compromise to the huge dilemma which lay before him. Liesel came back in from the garden, carrying the cat in her arms.

'Will you look after Mozart?' she asked softly.

'Of course. Whatever happens, Leez, please stay in touch. I couldn't bear it if you cut me out of your life. We've known each other since your parents died, and...'

'My *what*?'

Isaac cringed at the shocked look on her face.

'My parents died? Isaac? Is this true?'

'You better sit down, honey.'

'Did you know about this? Why didn't you tell me?' She was furious. 'You lied to me!'

'No, I didn't lie.'

She collapsed into his arms. Her face was white.

'I'll make us tea,' Jessica said, disappearing into the kitchen.

Jessica didn't like where this was heading. Instead, she tried to focus on the pleasant memories that they shared: all the Tuesday-night curries she cooked here in this tiny space with Liesel. And Saturday-morning pancakes, and Sunday brunches where they always had no less than fifteen musician friends around.

They'd first met on the day of Liesel's debut performance at the Opera House. They were up against each other in a competition for outstanding talent. Long before Liesel was notified of her parents' accident, Jessica was consoling her, wiping away her tears, and assuring her that, yes, her parents did love her, and they must have had a perfectly valid reason for not being in the audience. And yes, she was a brilliant violinist. That they weren't there didn't mean they thought she wasn't good enough.

The trauma of that day changed Jessica's life forever. Liesel became her best friend, and surrogate sister. Not a day went by when they didn't see each other or talk on the phone. Jessica decided against being a solo violinist, and chose instead the hub of an orchestra. They were, though, inseparable. By eighteen years of age, they were renting a house together.

'Why didn't Duncan tell me? Why didn't you tell me?' Liesel was beside herself. 'I don't even remember them. Who were they?'

'I can't answer that. You have those answers within you, and some day you'll remember everything.'

'Is there anything else I should know?'

'I don't think so. Look, we've had a really long day. Let's go to the hotel. We've got to head to Auckland tomorrow, and we need to meet up with your agent and music teacher later to talk about your Brisbane concert at the end of the week. You need to stay rested. That's my priority for you right now.'

Jessica gave Liesel a long hug, and didn't want to let her go. 'I love you, Leez. Don't ever forget that.

You're my best friend.'

Liesel felt emotional, not because of any conscious memory, but because there was something comforting about hearing the words *I love you*.

Duncan must have been pressing redial every few minutes. Isaac was close to throwing his mobile phone into the Sydney Harbour. Even though he had to call him back before they left Sydney, Isaac decided: *not now, not while we're having a leisurely breakfast and admiring the city skyline at dawn. Not now.*

Their flight was at 1pm. Isaac agreed for Duncan to meet them at the airport.

Duncan tried hugging Liesel, but she pulled away. The look in her eyes said 'Back off!'

'I'm not giving up, Liesel. You're my girl. It kills me that you're travelling around with some stranger, and that you won't even let me hold you. It's wrong!'

'Isaac is not a stranger.'

Duncan looked back and forth between them. No, surely not? They weren't lovers? No. Liesel wasn't like that. She wouldn't have sex with a man she barely knew. Hell, she didn't even have sex with the man who was now supposed to be her husband.

'I'm coming back to Scotland. Once these concerts are over, we're going to find a way to get your memory back. I won't be leaving there until you're ready to come home and be my wife!' He thumped the table. 'You're mine, Liesel. Mine!'

As she cowered back, Isaac gently placed his hand at the base of her lower spine offering her subtle support.

'Duncan...' Isaac was about to tell him to leave

her alone, when the boarding request came over the speakers.

'Good luck with the rest of your concerts. I'd really like to be there for them. Is there no way that I....'

'No.'

'You really should try being nicer to him,' Isaac whispered as he strode away. 'Please.'

Liesel looked at him as if to say *I hope you're joking*. 'That man would have been married to me if he had his way. It makes my skin crawl.'

Dazzled

Liesel wowed yet another audience, and by the end of the evening she had no doubt that she was, indeed, a virtuoso and that her playing hadn't been a fluke, but an art and a well-developed skill. The New Zealand audience was rapturous, and demanded several encores. Liesel happily obliged. Afterwards, Isaac wrapped his arms around her.

'You never cease to amaze me. You were born to play that instrument.'

'You might be right,' she conceded when he lifted her off the floor.

Auckland was magical, and they dined on the harbourside for breakfast the following day. The relaxed ambience of the city's downtown waterfront, and the turquoise sea water, thrilled Liesel. The people were friendly, which helped her feel right at home.

'Why don't we take a walk through the Waitakere Ranges while we're here?'

'Sure,' she replied, deep in thought.

'What's on your mind, honey?'

'I don't know, really. I'm just processing people and places. There seems to be so much to take in.'

'There is a lot to take in. Try not to let it overwhelm you. As I keep saying, just live one moment at a time. That's all either of us can ask for.' Isaac held her hand, a small gesture of reassurance.

They travelled out of Auckland, and into the ranges. Together they marvelled at the rugged forest-covered terrain, and how the land dipped to the Waitemata and Kaipara harbours.

Liesel thanked Isaac for these recreational interludes between concerts, and said how much it helped her.

'Being in a hotel the whole time would have driven me crazy,' she said.

'Me too! Though I'm sure we could have filled in the time quite productively,' he said, scooping her into his arms and kissing her passionately. Liesel loved how he did that; how he held her so confidently, with pride and pleasure. It was never a chore for him when he kissed her; never an obligation: his whole heart beat in time with hers.

The rainforest was quietly restorative after her hectic schedule, and she took succour from the giant Kauri trees, waterfalls and wild deserted beaches. They spent the whole day exploring huge black sand dunes, and the towering headlands. The surf thundered in, entrancing them with its power. All day long he made her laugh until her sides hurt, and tears fell freely down her cheeks.

'This place is amazing. I want to live here!' she said, adamant it was the only place on Earth for her.

'So, you've given up on Bali then?'

'No, I want to live there too.'

'You're so easily pleased, Liesel.'

They walked, hand in hand, along the black sands of Piha beach towards an apricot-infused sunset of the late New Zealand Summer.

Today had been one of her favourite days since leaving Scotland, and she hoped that she'd always remember it. Isaac made her laugh so many times, and she knew without a doubt that she wanted this for the rest of her life.

'I am going to love you forever, you know, Isaac' she said, looking firmly in his eyes.

'I pray that is true,' he offered, lifting her into his arms. 'I pray that is true.'

A lone figure, sporting a backpack, said 'hello' as he walked passed them, and then turned around and asked 'Liesel? Liesel Eather, is that you?'

Liesel and Isaac swung around.

'Liesel, it *is* you! I thought it was you!' The tourist laughed, and raced over and swung his arms around her body.

Liesel jolted, and in a moment of panic looked over to Isaac for reassurance.

'Isaac?'

The young man looked confused when she didn't acknowledge him.

'My mistake. I'm sorry. You look *exactly* like someone I met in Europe two months ago. Please forgive me. I didn't mean to scare you.'

Isaac intervened. 'It's no mistake. This is Liesel, but, I'm afraid...she lost her memory in Europe, and doesn't remember anything from her past.'

'Holy cow! Is that true? Oh man. I'm so sorry. I must have scared you to death. I really am so sorry.' With sensitivity and awareness, he stepped back a few paces to give her space.

Liesel relaxed a little and sensed he was genuine and warm.

'How do I know you?' she asked.

'We met in Mitten Wald, a little mountain village near Bavaria. It was at the Geigenbau museum. There are violins on display from the past few centuries.'

Isaac laughed. 'That sounds like just the sort of place Liesel would have visited!'

Liesel smiled, but didn't say anything as she studied the man carefully.

'I didn't know the first thing about violins,' he laughed 'but popped in to have a look while I was travelling through. You chewed my ear off. Liesel, you were a walking encyclopaedia on violins; how they're made, what they sound like, their history. You knew everything there was to know. I certainly got my money's worth that day.' He scratched his head. 'You do remember about the violins, don't you?'

She shook her head.

'She's an incredible violinist. I can't believe...'

'Liesel doesn't remember anything. My name's Isaac, pleased to meet you. I don't suppose you'd like to join us in the city for dinner? It would be nice for you to fill in some of the blanks for Liesel. If you've got time, that is.'

'I'd love it! My name's Jacob Hennesy. Jake. Just call me Jake.'

'You sound Canadian, Jake. Is that where you're from?'

'Sure am. Vancouver. I've been travelling the world for the past twelve months. I head home in two weeks. It'll be a bit strange settling down to a nine-to-five routine after a year of absolute freedom and no alarm clocks.'

They dined at the Harbourside Grill, enjoying the casual atmosphere and waterside views.

Jake talked for some time about his various travels around the world, and Isaac steered him back to his time with Liesel.

'So, we met in the museum, and then agreed to go out for a bite to eat. We spent the next two weeks travelling together. We were inseparable. She's such great company, as I'm sure you know. That laugh of hers. Wow.'

Isaac had to ask. He had to know: 'So, were you lovers?'

Jake's face became deadly serious. He looked at Liesel, taking her in, and then answered Isaac's question after blowing out a long breath.

'Any man who had Liesel as his lover would be one lucky chap! She's funny, smart, kind, empathetic, thoughtful. She'd drive a man insane with her sexiness.'

Isaac couldn't bear it. Jealousy was seeping in at the edges.

'But no, she wasn't my lover,' he confessed, as if the truth was some sort of regret.

'Because she was engaged to Duncan?' Isaac asked.

Jake laughed out loud. 'I wouldn't have let that stop me, besides, her heart was never with him. More than once she told me that she was going to break up with him; she was just waiting to find the right words and the right time.'

'If I'm so damn wonderful,' Liesel asked, finally breaking her silence, 'why didn't you sleep with me?'

Isaac laughed out loud at how indignant she was about the situation.

Jake smiled at her, and held her hand. 'Isaac, did I mention she has quite a temper? Beautiful Liesel Eather, there is only one reason in the world that I didn't sleep with you: I'm gay.'

There was visible relief in Isaac's eyes.

'Oh,' she whispered.

'But if I wasn't, I can assure you that you wouldn't be sitting here now with another man! I'd have never let you go.'

They all chuckled.

A few glasses of wine later, Jake's curiosity got the better of him: 'What ever happened with Duncan? Did you dump him?'

Liesel looked at Isaac.

Isaac replied. 'It's a work in progress.'

'That sounds messy. The Liesel I knew didn't do messy. Things were pretty black and white for her, even though she was one of the most colourful people I've ever met. I hope that person comes back. She was spectacular. Liesel Eather dazzled me, and I will never forget her.'

Isaac decided he rather liked Jake, especially now that he was no threat on the love front!

They dined until the early hours, and then parted ways with Jake, exchanging contact details.

'I truly hope our paths cross again, Liesel,' he said, kissing each of her cheeks, European style. 'You're one hell of a lady! Nice meeting you, Isaac.'

'And you, Jake.' Isaac said, firmly shaking his hand.

'Goodbye,' Liesel said, taking him in and trying desperately to place him into her memory. But she couldn't. Nothing about her old life made sense or held meaning. She found it so darn frustrating. Who was she? What sort of life did she want for herself? What were her dreams?

Eumundi

It was a balmy thirty degrees Celsius. Queensland sunshine warmed their skin as the hotel porters placed their suitcases into the rental car. The Brisbane concert had been another stunning performance. There were countless requests for follow-up concerts, recording offers, and untold networking. Isaac made sure she didn't promise anything, but diligently took everyone's contact details. There were a number of media interviews for magazines, newspapers, television and radio.

'I thought we could do a bit of sightseeing while we're here. Queensland is quite nice this time of year.' Isaac said, holding her close.

'That sounds lovely,' she whispered.

'What's the matter?' he asked, sensing something wasn't quite right.

'The questions. All the questions that the journalists ask, well, they've unnerved me. They know more about my life than I do. I feel like an idiot when they're asking me about my past and there's nothing I can say.'

'The good journalists steered away from that and kept focused on the music. From some of the articles I've seen, they've done a great job. Don't fret about it.'

Isaac sensed that she was mulling it over and over in her mind, and for the next hour she barely said a word. Was she remembering? Did their questions trigger something? He was sure of it, but *what* was she remembering?

They travelled for more than 100 kilometres, and were driving along Memorial Drive, just before the small town of Eumundi. Liesel was taking in the views of the Glasshouse Mountains and landscape below. The fields were filled with sugarcane, and as they rounded a bend, Liesel gasped.

'What is it, honey?' he asked, slowing down.

'Can you stop the car?' She was holding her hand to her chest.

He pulled over, and asked her again.

'What's the matter?'

She pointed to a roadside cross, a memorial to someone who had died in a car accident.

Liesel got out of the car, and walked over to it. She read the name, and date of death: March 22nd, and the words RIP Dad.

'Why do I feel so sad? I don't know this person.'

'You don't need to know who he was to feel empathy. You've been given information about your past, and now your body is putting it into context. At the deepest level, your body knows about loss.'

'Am I always going to feel sad when I see a roadside cross?' she asked.

'Probably. It will always make you think of your parents. You'll always have a connection to every other person who has lost a loved one in this way. Honey, this is a good thing. Something is shifting inside you.'

'Do you think it's odd that my parents died in a car accident, and then I met you through one?'

'I wouldn't give it too much thought.'

He held her hand, and then led her back to the car. Isaac had hoped the visit to Eumundi might cheer her up.

It was market day, and the place was vibrant, and busy. Liesel loved the feel of the warm sunshine on her skin, and the scent of eucalyptus wafting through the market. They wandered by the stalls, stopping to learn more about herbal potions, tie-dye clothing, and to sample fresh, organic bread, cheese, and to drink good coffee. It was a world away, in every sense, to the life Isaac knew, but he was patient and trusting.

Wandering through the crowded open-air market amongst the park-side trees, they sipped a mango smoothie, chatted with the stallholders, and purchased hand-crafted jewellery, ginger beer and crafts.

Liesel was drawn to magnificent crystals, Tibetan singing bowls and aromatherapy oils.

'I'm never going to get you out of here,' Isaac laughed as he purchased freshwater pearl earrings, several Indian sarongs and far too much incense; but the smile on her face was worth it. Liesel seemed right at home in this alternative community. It certainly matched the wardrobe of hers that he'd witnessed in Sydney: she was a bohemian girl through and through.

They were savouring roasted-cinnamon macadamia nuts when they walked around the corner and came across a young girl busking on a violin.

Liesel stopped, and watched her play. For a while, she studied the young violinist's technique; her head tilting from one side to the other. The girl was struggling on a certain part of the piece.

When she'd finished performing, Liesel went up and whispered in her ear. The girl looked at her, then to her mother who was sitting on a nearby bench, and back to Liesel.

'Try it, I promise it will work,' Liesel urged.

The girl did as instructed, repeating a few bars from the piece. A huge smiled wrapped across her face.

'Wow. It works!' She looked at her mother, the

expression on the woman's face a mixture of pride and confusion.

'I used to get stuck on the exact same part all the time.'

'My teacher never explained it like you did. Now it feels easy,' the young girl giggled with delight.

'Well, I hope you never forget it. You're so talented.'

Isaac dropped a fifty dollar note into the opened violin case, and couldn't help but smile when the girl's eyes nearly popped out in disbelief at his generosity.

The child's mother wandered over, and said 'Thank you. Hatti loves that piece so much, but has always struggled with the 20th to 25th bar.'

'Well, she'll never struggle again,' Liesel laughed. 'Fifth position is really hard, but this technique will help you with accuracy and tone. Work on that double-stopping, thirds and glissando and you'll never look back. You're so much better than you think you are. Truly. You've got so much talent. Hatti, you are going to go a long way.'

'Are you the lady who was on the news? The virtuoso who has been touring the country?'

'Yes, I am. Liesel Eather. Pleased to meet you,' she said, reaching out her hand.

The young mother bit her lip nervously, then asked: 'Hatti has a recital tomorrow afternoon. I don't suppose you're free to offer moral support? I know it's a long shot, a huge imposition really, it's just that her teacher is off sick...'

'Of course I could. That'd be alright, wouldn't it Duncan?' she said, turning around to check with him.

'Isaac. I'm *Isaac*, not Duncan.'

In that moment, he didn't recognise his own voice.

It was low, distant, raspy, pained. No. Not now. Not here. Not like this!

Isaac wanted to stop time. No damn it, he wanted to turn back time.

His deepest desire for her, and his greatest fear for himself: yes, right here, right now. The world he had been building with and for Liesel was crumbling around him. Around them. At this point, he had no idea how much of her memory had returned, but as he watched her with the young girl, coaching her through a piece, he knew, just knew, that the bubble they were living in was bursting before his eyes. Calling him 'Duncan' just confirmed it. This was, without question, the most terrifying moment of his life. It was worse than the first day of boarding school, and the subsequent years spent there; worse than his mother leaving and disappearing from his life; worse than inheriting a run-down, debt-ridden castle; worse than identifying his father's drowned body at the edge of the loch, and worse than his late wife tripping down the staircase when she was drunk. Worse. Worse. *Worse.*

Liesel was his *life*. Everything that had been of value to him was now irrelevant without her there by his side. He needed her! Isaac needed her smile, her laughter, her boldness, her joy, her effervescence. Without her, he was dead.

'Isaac,' she said, not so much as a question but as an affirmation.

For a few seconds, her face was blank, and then she smiled broadly, melting his heart quicker than the Australian sunshine on a lump of ice. 'Isaac!' She reached up and kissed him, and asked 'Can we make time to go to Hatti's rehearsal?'

'Absolutely,' he said, nodding at the girl and

squeezing Liesel's hand tightly. What could he do to make sure she never left his side? His mind was racing.

First, he wrote down the address and time, and promised they'd be there, then he guided Liesel away from the market and back to the rental car. The beat of his heart warned of impending danger.

They spent the night at Jacaranda Creek Bed and Breakfast. It was a sanctuary from their nights in major cities, and they enjoyed strolling the 23-acre farmland, feeding the alpacas and ponies. They hadn't spoken about her calling him Duncan, or how much she remembered. Liesel had been relatively quiet for the rest of the afternoon, and went to sleep early that night. In the morning, she simply smiled and said what a beautiful day it was.

Isaac invited her for another walk, and they headed down towards the large pond.

'The eucalyptus trees smell incredible,' she said, taking a deep breath and closing her eyes. The stormbird called from a distance, and a kookaburra laughed in reply.

Liesel's shoe scuffed at the red soil beneath her feet. She knew she couldn't avoid the subject any longer.

'I'm so sorry I called you Duncan. I can't explain what happened. I was helping Hatti, and I knew the piece she played so well. Duncan was always so patient when I played. And I played a lot. Generally, I would play for eight hours a day. He never complained, and was happy to be second best. He knew that the violin was my great love. Although he was tolerant of my rehearsal time, Duncan got irritated when I stopped to help children who were busking. I couldn't help myself. Very often they just needed to adjust a technique, and they were usually things that could be remedied. More often than not, they could mean the difference between a child quitting music lessons or going on to become brilliant musicians. He said I spent far too much time helping strangers rather than being with him. Duncan insisted that when I was out with him, I had to focus only on him.'

'You need to phone him, Liesel. Duncan needs to know that you remember, and…and you need to make a decision.'

'What decision?'

'You need to decide if you're going to stay with me or go back to Duncan.'

'There is no choice, Isaac. I choose you.'

'You can't know this. You need to see him again. You need to know how you feel now that your memory is back.'

'*You* are my memory. Whatever we've been sharing; this is my life now. *With you*. I don't want to go back to my past.'

'So you don't feel any differently towards me? You're not uncomfortable when I touch you, when I kiss you?' he asked, bringing her in closer and letting his lips meet hers.

They lingered for a while, as if he was scared to let her answer. His thoughts raced to how she went straight to sleep the night before.

'I love you more than ever. If I'm quiet, if I'm non-communicative, it's because there is so much going on in my mind. I'm trying to integrate everything I remember, from the past and from recent times with you, and where we've been together. I'm putting my past with my present, and trying to assemble my future. Of course I have feelings for Duncan,' she said, 'He's been in my life for as long as I can remember. He was always at my side. But...well, the feelings I have for him are different to the ones I have for you. I can't explain it, except to say that I want to stay with you.'

Liesel moved away from him, then asked 'Do you feel differently towards me? Has the novelty worn off? Does the idea of being with the real me not seem so exotic now? Do you just want to go back to your cave and leave me here?' Her voice was trembling, and she held back her tears.

'Of course my feelings haven't changed. But... Liesel, you were never mine. You were always Duncan's girl. I,' he choked on his words. 'I have to set you free.'

Like an animal in pain, she cried out.

'Why would you say that? That's cruel!'

'No, it's not cruel. It's the truth. I need to set you free to return to your old life...to Duncan. And if you can honestly say that you don't want to be with him, then I will absolutely, one hundred percent, have you in my life. Surely you must understand that there can be no other way?'

'No! I don't understand. I don't!' Liesel ran away from him into an area of thick scrubland looking for space to cry. And there, she fell to her knees, her bare skin grazed against the dry red soil.

Isaac wanted to rush to her side. It was wrong to do this to her; to the woman he loved. But what choice did he have? It was unethical not to at least give Liesel and Duncan another chance. The man was meant to be married to her by now!

Liesel barely spoke a word all day. Isaac drove her to Hatti's recital, and they sat at the back of the audience for the duration.

'That was simply wonderful, Hatti!' Liesel said,

congratulating her afterwards. 'You had nothing to worry about.'

They talked for a while, and Hatti shared her plans about becoming a world-famous performer. She talked quickly, and said it was in her blood. Hatti's mother confided that it was hard to find a good teacher where they lived, and she wondered if it was worth moving to another location.

'Well, the right teacher is important. It's not just about the knowledge they pass on, but the chemistry between teacher and student. It's a relationship based on trust, inspiration, encouragement and mutual dreams. The teacher needs to feel just as passionate about their student's dreams as the student does.'

'Who was your teacher, Liesel?'

'I had several teachers. My favourite was Vissimo, but she was only here in Australia for two years, then she returned to Italy because, would you believe, she met her soulmate and followed him to Florence! In fairness, she was from Florence anyway.'

'That sounds so romantic.'

'It was. It is. They're a lovely couple, and two of my favourite people in the whole world.'

'Does Vissimo still play violin?'

'Actually, she does. And, lucky for her, Jack does too. They teach teenage violinists in Italy.'

'Wow. That's sounds so cool.'

Isaac listened in, and despite his aching heart, he couldn't help smiling. Liesel was such a natural with children, but it was her affection for Jack and Vissimo which really tugged at him. They were her family bond. Now that her memory was coming back, there was so much to learn about her, and about the people in her life. Liesel hadn't said much because of how upset she was, but he hoped she would start sharing her life story with him.

He wanted to know everything about her, and he didn't want to wait much longer. But first, she had to tell Duncan. It was only right that he knew.

'Here's my address,' Hatti said, slipping a piece of paper into Liesel's hands. 'I want you to come to one of my concerts when I'm famous. Will you be my pen friend?'

'I promise!' Liesel said, giving the girl a huge hug. 'It's such a delight to know you, Hatti.'

Hatti's mum embraced Liesel. 'I can't tell you what a gift you've given her. Truly, that simple bit of advice at the market will change her life.'

They parted ways, and Liesel wiped a tear from her eye.

'If only all relationships were that easy,' she whispered, knowing the task which lay ahead.

Isaac suggested they take a walk on the beach at Caloundra before she called Duncan. He held her hand, trying to bridge the emotional gap that the day had brought.

'I only want the best for you, Liesel. Only the best,' he promised, looking away from her and out to sea so that she didn't witness his watery eyes.

'I know.'

Reluctantly, they headed back to their accommodation.

'Duncan, it's Liesel. My...my memory has returned.'

'*Babe*!!!!!! Babe, that's fantastic news. When are you coming back? Shall I come and meet you? Where are you?'

'Don't call me babe!' She was furious.

Isaac couldn't help but smile from behind the other side of the newspaper.

'But babe, you used to love it when I called you babe.'

'I never liked it. It's demeaning. I just never said anything because I wanted to keep the peace. Look, we're travelling up to the far north of Queensland, and then flying out of Brisbane. We can meet at the airport before I leave, if you like?'

'What do you mean? Are you out of your mind? This is crazy! You should be flying back to me, planning to reschedule our wedding. What sort of hold does this Heathfield bloke have on you anyway? Please don't tell me you've fallen in love with him?'

There was nothing but silence as he waited for her answer.

Liesel looked over at Isaac who was reading the newspaper review about her recent concerts.

'Yes, I'm in love with Isaac Heathfield. I'm sorry, Duncan.' She spoke coolly, but with tenderness, her eyes never once straying from Isaac.

Isaac's eyes widened in disbelief at her confession.

'Liesel, I'm coming straight up to Queensland. We have to sort this mess out!'

Liesel raised her eyebrows in exasperation. 'There's nothing to sort out, Duncan.' Reluctantly, she ended up giving him details of where they'd be staying in the far north, and agreed to catch up the next day.

'Did you really have to tell him that news over the phone? It's a pretty devastating thing to share. It would have been better in person.' Isaac suggested.

'In person, I'd have to look into his eyes and watch his pain. It was better not to be caught up in that.'

'You're a hard woman,' Isaac said, shaking his head.

They caught a chartered flight to Airlie Beach, and settled in to their accommodation.

'Let's go out to dinner. In case this is our last night together, let's make it special,' he said softly, his voice raw and pained.

'Last night?' It was unthinkable. She felt like a lamb being marched through a slaughterhouse: vulnerable, innocent. Her life was in someone else's hands. Electrodes of pain shook her heart. It felt like her future was not her own. Terror ripped through her veins. How could Isaac just let her walk away?

Cha'mah, a Moroccan-inspired restaurant, overlooked the water. Isaac chose outside seating so the sea breeze could offer respite from the relentless humidity. Candles flickered, and soft music played in the background. Each table had a small plant, and the restaurant itself was a jungle of ferns and palms, lending a peaceful atmosphere. Coloured fabrics swayed in the breeze, and small lanterns added muted light. Brightly coloured silk and sequined cushions adorned the seating. The walls were washed in a light-terracotta colour.

Liesel chose dukkah, a mixture of herbs, nuts and spices, served with olive oil and Turkish bread, followed by buckwheat pancakes with warm goats' cheese, and sweet chutney. Isaac chose the Moroccan potato soup with wild thyme, then spicy eggplant and a pumpkin tagine. Conversation was light. Meaningless, really. It felt as if they were just filling in time while waiting for the inevitable parting of ways.

Isaac's phone rang. 'Okay,' he said, putting his fork down. 'We're just on the waterside. *Cha'mah*.' He reached for Liesel's hand.

'He's coming here?' She stood up, as if about to run away.

'Honey, sit down. We have to face this. We *always* had to face this moment. Let's get it over and done with so we all know where we stand.'

'But tonight was supposed to be about us. About me and you. Not about him!'

'Liesel, you loved Duncan. You were meant to marry him.'

'You're wrong. I never loved him!'

'How can you say that?' Isaac could see she was getting distraught, and he stood up and put his arms around her. 'I love you, Liesel, and the price I pay for that is allowing you to have free will.'

'This *is* my will! My will is *you*! Don't make me go back to him.'

'I'm not making you do anything, honey, I just want you to talk to him. To see him face to face and trust your feelings.'

'I do trust my feelings, and that's why I'm here with you.'

What Isaac really wanted was for her to be absolutely clear that she only wanted to be with him. That could only happen if she spent some time with Duncan. Every second disappeared in haste. Isaac desperately wanted to halt time.

Within ten minutes, Duncan arrived at the restaurant. Nervously, he adjusted his tie, then locking his rental car he walked over to their table. Today he cut a striking figure in his suit, a far cry from the casual clothes he usually wore. Duncan and Isaac acknowledged each other with a minimal head nod. 'Do you think I might have some time alone with my fiancée?' Duncan asked, finding his testosterone.

'I'm not your fiancée. The wedding was cancelled.'

'Postponed,' he argued. 'Just postponed until you got your memory back.'

Isaac stood up, trying hard to ignore the look of fear on Liesel's face. 'I'll just be down by the boats. I won't be far away. I promise.' It was all he could do not to hold her, to tell her everything would be okay. That tomorrow they'd fly back to Scotland. But he couldn't tell her that. No, Isaac couldn't promise her anything.

'Isaac?' she cried. 'Don't leave me.'

'I'm just going to the boats, Liesel,' he said, pointing to the marina.

Walking away from her was the hardest thing he ever had to do in his life. Liesel had turned up on his property like a lightning bolt, and struck him without warning. It had never been his intention to fall in love with her, with anyone. Truth was, he'd found contentment living as a virtual hermit in his castle, writing books. Over time he'd learnt that he didn't need anyone. How could she have changed his life so quickly?

One last time, he looked back, just to check she was okay. Their eyes met, and lightning struck. It hurt! Damn it. Love shouldn't be painful.

'Babe,' Duncan said, reaching out to touch her hand. She pulled away.

'Don't call me babe. It's irritating. Childish.'

'But babe...'

Liesel stood up, ready to scream.

'I'm sorry. Just a force of habit.'

'Duncan, whatever we had, it's over. I'm sorry if that hurts. We were in each other's lives for so long, and while it's true we were going to get married, everything has changed.'

'Not for me it hasn't. You're still the woman I want to marry!'

'Even if I don't feel the same way?'

'Of course you love me. You've just transferred your feelings to Heathfield because he rescued you.'

'When have I ever said that I loved you?'

It was a simple question, but the enormity of it nearly threw Duncan off his chair.

Liesel watched the panic on his face as he searched his memory banks.

'What do you mean? You said yes when I asked you to marry me!'

'When have I ever said *I love you*?'

'Why did you agree to marry me?'

'It felt safe. I have no family...I...I don't know! We've known each other so long; it just seemed the obvious thing to do.'

When Liesel began to cry, she picked up the linen napkin to wipe her tears. Duncan stood up, and walked around to her. Instinctively, he put his arms around Liesel.

'Please don't,' she cried. 'I'm sorry if I'm hurting you, but this is over.'

'Liesel, you've been...well, it's like you've been hypnotised. You're not thinking straight. Surely you must remember all the fun times we've had together?'

'Yes, they were fun,' she had to admit. 'But what I feel for you is different. It's more platonic. Our relationship was based on friendship.'

'We can change that. We can change it tonight. Give me a chance. Don't throw everything away because you haven't experienced what else we could have.'

Liesel searched his eyes. Why was this so hard? Her feelings for him couldn't even be compared to what she felt for and with Isaac.

'No,' she said softly. 'I don't want to do that.'

'You're not even giving me a chance. This isn't right, Liesel. This isn't fair!'

After she finished crying, Duncan convinced her to leave the restaurant and go for a walk. They headed down to the beach, walking in the opposite direction from Isaac.

'Has all of your memory returned?' Duncan asked.

'Yes. I think so. Why?' she looked at him, unsure of what he was getting at.

'You're so hostile towards me. I understand you falling for Isaac, especially given the circumstances. I do. What I don't understand is why I'm the enemy. When did all this change? Don't you remember I was the one there for you when you crashed?'

'Crashed?' she asked, wondering what he meant. 'Car accident?'

'When you had your nervous breakdown, Leez. Your black depression which lasted two solid years? Don't you remember that? Your descent into living hell! Liesel, it was me who sat by your side every day when you didn't have the strength to walk outside. It was me who stuck by you, not Isaac Heathfield. Me!'

'I was depressed? Me?'

'You don't remember?'

She looked at him blankly. 'I thought all my memory was back, but I have no idea what you're talking about.'

'You have to give us a chance, Liesel. Don't throw away what we had. Not yet. Not without trying.'

'I'm sorry the wedding was cancelled, Duncan,' she apologised softly, her voice carrying on the sea breeze.

'Postponed, babe, just postponed. We can set a new date,' he assured her.

'I'm not saying I want that,' Liesel said firmly, 'I'm simply apologising. I'm sorry for the hurt I've brought into your life. I'd do anything to change that. You're a good man. I know that. You're kind and caring. You don't deserve what I've put you through.'

'Stop putting me through it, then. Come back to Sydney. Meet up with Julia again, and let's get you performing.'

They spent several minutes in silence, looking out to sea.

'I don't want to perform!' she said, feeling angry.

'You were born to perform.'

'No, Duncan. That's why I became depressed.'

'I thought you didn't remember being depressed?' he asked, completely confused by their conversation.

'I didn't, but I do now. You were kind to me. I remember you being attentive, and never leaving my side. You were patient, loving, tolerant. I didn't deserve you.'

'Don't go down that track, Liesel. Of course you deserve me. We deserve each other! Now, let's send Heathfield home to Scotland, we can go back and resume our life in Sydney. What do you say, babe?' Although his voice was soft, and she could see he desperately cared, her heart was tearing in two.

'I love Isaac.'

'Maybe you just think you do. I can only begin

to imagine the shock of waking up in some strange bloke's home in the middle of nowhere. It was probably a protection mechanism to identify with him; a way of feeling safe.'

'No, Duncan.' Tears fell from her eyes. 'It wasn't like that at all. With Isaac, as soon as I saw him, it was like I was alive for the first time in my life.'

'You're not thinking straight. It's such a ridiculous thing to say. What about all the good times we've had together? Babe, you have to give us a chance. Come back to Sydney. Give me two weeks to remind you of what we had. If you can honestly walk away from that without a backwards glance, then I'll not hold you back. I promise.'

Liesel felt his gentle hand on hers.

'Okay. I'll give it two weeks,' she offered, smiling weakly. What she really wanted to do was run back to Isaac's arms, and to feel safe. But she also knew that she couldn't live with herself if she didn't give him a chance. Surely he deserved at least that from her?

Duncan threw his arms around Liesel, and lifted her off the sand; he was about to kiss her when Isaac came into view, walking swiftly towards them.

When Duncan groaned, she asked 'What's wrong?'

'Heathfield's coming.'

Liesel turned around, and one look into his eyes had her heart leaping. She smiled at him, as if the whole world was suddenly a beautiful place again. But his eyes didn't reflect her joy.

Isaac was desperately trying to read her; read them. The energy between them was different to when he'd left them in the restaurant. Why did she let Duncan hug her?

'Babe's coming back with me to Sydney.' Duncan announced triumphantly.

The colour disappeared from Isaac's face.

'Just for two weeks,' Liesel assured him. 'I'm going back for two weeks, that's all.'

Isaac knew that despite wanting to carry her off the beach and away from this situation, he had to let her do this. If she came straight back to Scotland, he'd spend the rest of his life wondering what if, and she most certainly would, too.

'Okay. Where are you going to stay? Your belongings have all been packed up. Jess was planning to rent your room out.'

'She can stay with me,' Duncan said.

'I don't think that's a good idea,' Isaac replied.

'Why? She's my fiancée. My home is her home!'

Isaac looked into Liesel's eyes. 'She needs space while she makes her decision. Liesel needs a place of her own each day to process whatever is coming up for her. If she's with you all day long, and each...' The words choked in his mouth. Isaac wanted to say: Nights with Liesel belong to me, not you! 'She needs space at night. What do you think, Liesel?'

'I think you're right. I need...'

'I'll book you a suite at the Shangri La. Two weeks, two months....you take all the time you need. All I ask is that you check in with me each day and let me know how you're doing. Can you do that?'

Liesel tried to contain the tears flowing from her eyes. This was all so wrong! Everything in her body wanted to shout out and tell the world how very much she loved Isaac Heathfield, and how she wanted to have children with him, and hide away at Stoneyhill Castle for the rest of their lives. But here, with Duncan holding her hand, she could hardly say that. All she could do, all she did, was pull away from him and reclaim her own space.

'Of course I can,' she said.

Isaac reached up to wipe the tears from her eyes. When his skin touched hers, lightning struck. There was no choice to make, so why the hell was she going to walk away?

Duncan pulled out a handkerchief and passed it to her.

'Here babe, wipe your tears. You can fly back to Sydney with me tonight. By the way, some guy named Kam Mitchell phoned Julia about you doing a concert back there. You can use my phone to call him when we leave. Now, let's go and get your bags.'

They started walking up the beach towards their accommodation when Liesel ran back to Isaac and threw her arms around his neck. 'I love you, Isaac Heathfield. No matter what happens, never ever forget that.'

It was her turn to wipe tears from his cheek.

'No matter what happens?'

'No matter what happens…' she said.

Did she doubt that they'd get back together? Did she really think, even for a small moment, that she might choose Duncan over Isaac?

Isaac reluctantly let her go, and watched her walk up the beach with Duncan, torment in every step. *No matter what happens.* What the hell did that mean?

Panic coursed through his veins. Why did he agree to this? First, she'd turned his ordered life upside down, and now it was being turned inside out. Every second of this ordeal was a nightmare. One thing was clear: he should never have let her into his life, or into his heart.

Harmonic Notes

It felt like the longest night of Isaac's life, and he desperately wanted Liesel by his side. Although he'd booked her an adjoining suite at the Shangri La in Sydney, as promised, what he didn't know was if she'd checked in. As much as it went against the grain, he refrained from visiting her, and trusted that she'd be in touch with him each day, as agreed. Isaac tossed, turned, twisted.

The next day was the slowest on record. Isaac hung around the foyer, hoping to catch a glimpse of her but she must have left the hotel early that morning. It was almost nine that night when he saw her arrive through the front doors. To his mind, she looked wrung out; thoroughly exhausted. Liesel wore her hair in two braids, and it wiped ten years off her looks. Isaac's heart pounded at the innocent vision. When their eyes met, a powerful force catapulted between them. It split the atmosphere, like an applause from the gods.

Isaac had felt flat all day, but now his senses were sharpened. Awed by her beauty, fearful at what lay ahead, he moved closer. Liesel was too far away, and he needed to change that.

Vigilant for any sign of danger, he stepped towards her. There was no indication that Duncan was accompanying her. A brilliant white light shattered the air between them, climaxing in an almighty roar. Thunder rumbled as they fell into each other's arms. At long last, they were back together. She'd been gone too long, and he hadn't liked it one bit.

Liesel felt as if she'd just sought shelter from a storm. A storm so vicious it threatened her very existence. 'I don't feel in control of my life,' she whispered, breathing in his scent: cedar and spice. Just smelling his skin made her remember everything about their relationship. She wanted to stay here forever, with him, in this holy place of their bodily embrace. 'You smell amazing,' she whispered. 'You smell like home. I feel safe again just being in your arms.'

'You're the most powerful person I've ever met. You can get through this,' he promised. 'Of course you're in control. That power you feel? That lightning which burns between us? It's the force of life. It can only harm you if you don't follow your heart. When you make your choice, whether it's me or Duncan, then this energy won't feel so frightening.'

'You make it sound so easy,' she cried.

'Come with me,' he said, leading her to a quiet table in the corner of the empty reception area. 'I can't take you back to my room, as much as I'd do anything to have you in my bed. It's not fair. I have to abide by this agreement. But this I know: you're in touch with your intuition, and the messages from your body. Listen to that. Stop listening to your head. Listen to your heart.'

'If I listen to my heart, there is no choice. It's only you. Isaac, you're the only one I ever want to be with.' Liesel looked at him thoughtfully. 'You're the only man I've ever been with...' She didn't finish the sentence. 'But my head? Oh my head! I *know* Duncan. I've known him for a large part of my life. He's seen me through some difficult times. As much as I love you, I hardly know you. How do I sustain a relationship with you when...'

'We know each other, Liesel. We *know* each other.

Don't doubt that for a second. You're the one who showed me that. You convinced me of that. Of course we know each other. We may not know things like each other's favourite colour or whether we're cat or dog people, but we know things that really matter. We know each other in ways that go beyond words. The rest of those details are ones we can spend our lives discovering.'

'Isaac, we've made love to each other. Of course it's going to give us something that I don't have with Duncan. You see, I've never…'

Liesel wasn't sure how to tell him. 'I've never made love with Duncan. I insisted we waited till our wedding night. That was mostly a diversion tactic.'

'I know that I was your first. I overheard Duncan talking about you saving yourself for marriage. How do you feel about that?'

'I don't know.' She sighed, and looked a little sheepish. 'Do you know why I went to Europe?'

'To travel?' he smiled.

'To escape. I feel so embarrassed sharing this but I found myself planning a wedding I had no desire at being part of. I…you're going to think I'm so fickle.'

'Never mind what I think! Just tell me.'

'I didn't want to marry Duncan. Not really. He was there. He was the one consistent thing in my life.'

'What about your violin?'

'My violin scared me! There was nothing safe or consistent about that. It was truly a love-hate relationship. There was so much pressure on me to perform. I spiralled into depression, never leaving my room. I played. I played every day. It was my solace, but it didn't feel safe. It felt like walking on a cliff edge every day. I had two years of blackness. It truly was black. Duncan was with me throughout. I was unable to go out to work. For the next few years after that, he was always there. Always kind, devoted, determined. Isaac, I feel like I owe him. Duncan gave up years of his life to support me. My inheritance was squandered on sustaining me through illness.'

'I appreciate that. But does this mean you give up the rest of your life in order to make things even?'

'I don't know what it means. I promised him two weeks. That's the least I can do, surely?'

'Of course it is. Just be careful, Liesel. Listen to your heart, not your head. Promise me.'

'I promise,' she said, reaching out to touch his hand. They both pulled away instantly, the spark almost scorching them. 'I promise,' she said again, catching her breath. 'I want to come to bed with you. I want to go home with you. Every cell in my being wants to be with you. This isn't fair!'

'It certainly doesn't seem fair,' he said, kicking the leg of the stool. 'What plans do you have tomorrow?'

'Duncan wants me to meet some guy about playing at a private function.'

'Will you meet me here tomorrow night?'

'Yes, honey, I promise,' she smiled weakly, reaching out her hand again.

Would it be wrong for them to go back to Scotland tonight? Would it be wrong to just disappear and start their lives together as if her past didn't exist?

Liesel felt the music of her ancestresses around her; the vibrations and rhythms which had helped them survive, were now embracing her, urging her to be strong. *Listen to the harmony*, she heard them whisper down the generations. *Ignore the dissonance, and feel the sensations. Your life can be a symphony.*

'I'm sorry you were depressed,' he said softly. 'And I'm glad Duncan was there for you. I understand why you can't walk away. Not everyone who suffers mental illness has the luxury of a supportive person in their life.'

'I know.'

'How long were you on medication?'

'I was never on any. I tried to deal with it naturally. I used St John's wort. Some days it worked okay, and I could function enough to get dressed and eat and play violin in my room. Duncan tried to have me committed to a psychiatric ward. I can't blame him. He was at his wit's end. Jess stepped in. She refused to let it happen. Bless her, she spent hours researching natural cures. What helped me in the end was transdermal-magnesium therapy. It was natural, and just what I needed. Once my magnesium levels returned to normal, I was able to start thinking clearly and functioning like a human being and to start eating again. I verged on anorexia for a long time. It can be one of the symptoms of magnesium deficiency, and my nutritional status was depleted from all the stress I'd been through. And oddly, once my magnesium levels returned to healthy, it helped my nervousness and anxiety hugely. Without it, I'd never have been able to agree to the concerts. It saved my life.'

'So, let's be clear: *magnesium* saved your life, not Duncan?'

She smiled. 'I think you're right.'

Duncan drove well beyond the city hoping to distract her from any thoughts about Isaac. The plan was to take Liesel bushwalking in the Blue Mountains. He'd packed a picnic for later in the day. After trekking for a few hours, Liesel stopped to marvel at the sandstone gorges and plateaux which were dominated by forests of eucalypt. They settled by a waterfall, and ate their lunch. He spoke of their life together, and highlighted shared memories. Duncan enjoyed watching her laugh. He'd missed her so much. When she was healthy, she was always such fun company. Liesel was his best friend.

There was no arguing that it had been a pleasant day, and she was grateful that he went out of his way to make it so memorable. 'Babe, we can have plenty more days like this. You just have to let me back into your heart.'

Isaac and Liesel met each evening in the foyer of Shangri La, talking about their day. On the fifth day, Liesel said 'I'm playing at a private party tomorrow night. I only agreed because it's small. About 15 people. Strangely, I don't feel nervous.'

'Is Duncan going with you?'

'No. I'm going on my own. I won't be able to meet you tomorrow night. I'll be back too late. I'm sorry.'

'I will miss you.'

'Me too. More than you could ever know.'

Missing Pieces

Liesel dressed in a violet and indigo velvet dress which draped in layers, and had tiny buttons all the way down the front. For her footwear, she chose Italian pumps, and selected a matching handbag. When she arrived at the estate, on a vineyard just outside of Sydney, she stopped to admire the view before her. It was sunset, and the light across the vines looked magnificent. The hostess, Alice, had arranged a limousine for her. They'd not met beforehand, as event had been arranged by a third party: Kam Mitchell; a close friend of her agent.

Liesel stepped out, and walked up the front steps of the palatial mansion. A maid greeted her at the door.

'I'm here to see Alice,' Liesel said softly. Perhaps she felt nervous after all; with a flutter in her belly, she was unsure of how the evening would play out.

'Come this way, madam.'

Liesel followed her through several spacious rooms. Guests had already arrived and were sipping champagne.

The maid knocked on the door.

'Come in.'

Liesel walked through, and felt somewhat abandoned when the maid left her alone.

'I'm Liesel Eather. You've booked me to play tonight.'

The lady was well dressed, in a beautiful white pant suit. Both elegant and graceful, Liesel was immediately drawn to her. There was a faint familiarity to her, and she smiled instantly when their eyes met. But there was nothing in Liesel's past that she could remember. No, she was sure they hadn't met but she felt so at home when she looked into the lady's eyes.

Odd, she was sure they'd never met before.

'Liesel, I'm so glad you agreed to do this. My name's Alice. I saw you play at the opera house. You were amazing.'

'It's my pleasure to be here, Mrs?...'

'Just Alice. Come this way. Perhaps you'll have time to chat later on, after you've performed?'

'Of course. What are you celebrating, Alice?'

Alice turned to her, and touched Liesel's hand. 'Coming home. Coming home.'

'Where have you been?' Liesel asked curiously.

'Nowhere, and everywhere. We'll talk later,' she promised.

This was Liesel's first performance since her memory returned. It felt like a safe environment: small, intimate, and with friendly guests. Perhaps she could play again, and enjoy it. Maybe, she could craft a life for herself where performance anxiety was manageable. She didn't need to be a superstar. What if she chose functions like this?

The experience felt completely different, on many levels, to her concerts; and not just because her memory had returned. This was like playing for a few friends, even though she didn't recognise their faces. Their smiles guided her through. There were several favourites which she always included when she played. She read through her list before picking up the bow.

Sibelius Concerto, 3rd movement
Paganini Caprices
Bach Chaconne
Mendelssohn E minor

St. Saens Concerto No. 2
Carmen Fantasy
Paganini Concerto No.2
Symphonie Espagnole

With all her heart, she wished that Isaac was here to watch her perform. He'd be so proud of her; she knew that. A tear glistened at the edge of her eye as she thought of him, and of how he'd turned his whole life on its axis so he could help her find her life again. And what was her life? Who was she really? What was the life she had here? What did it mean if Isaac wasn't part of it? The idea was unthinkable. But Duncan had been so attentive to her, and with each passing day she realised why she'd chosen to say yes to his marriage proposal: he cared for her.

The applause was addictive, and she had to admit that part of her did enjoy audience appreciation. Mostly, though, she loved to play for herself and become one with the music, rather than be distracted by other people's experiences of the sounds which sang from her instrument.

'Liesel, you were incredible. Somehow this night was just perfect.' Alice held her hand. 'It's late. Can you stay the night? I have plenty of guest rooms. We look to be the same clothing size, so I could lend you some clothing if you like.'

'Alice, that's generous, but there's no need.'

'Please. I...I have something I'd like to discuss with you. It's a bit late now, but perhaps if you stay we could talk in the morning. It's important.'

The look in her eyes told Liesel that she couldn't refuse. Shouldn't refuse. Whatever it was that was so important, she had to stay.

'Okay. I need to make a couple of phone calls.'

Liesel wandered out into the dark night. Standing beneath the stars she took out her mobile, and phoned Duncan, saying that she wouldn't be able to meet up tomorrow. Unsurprisingly, he wasn't happy at all, but said they could meet up at the Noodle Bar the following day.

'I'm so glad it went well, honey,' Isaac said reassuringly. She could hear the tiredness in his voice. 'I've missed you tonight. Really missed you.'

'Me too. See you tomorrow night?'

'I wouldn't miss it for the world.' When she ended the call, her heart felt more at peace than when she'd said goodbye to Duncan. They'd each responded so differently to her.

Alice greeted Liesel with a nightcap, then showed her to her room.

'Breakfast is at eight, but if you prefer to sleep in, then don't worry. The maid can bring you something to your room. Otherwise, I'll meet you out in the back garden for breakfast. I've left some clothes and toiletries in your room. Wear whatever you like.'

'You're so kind to me, Alice. I don't know what I've done to deserve this, but thank you.'

'Everything about you deserves this, Liesel. Everything.'

Liesel had no idea what she meant, but she sensed the lady was authentic.

Liesel slept soundly, to her great surprise. She'd expected to toss and turn; to reach for Isaac. But when she awoke, it was to the sound of her own voice calling Duncan's name, and her face was awash with salty tears. Duncan? She asked herself. Why call for Duncan? It was Isaac she wanted. Not Duncan.

Washing away those thoughts, she took a long shower in the ensuite, and then dressed in jeans and a simple orange blouse, and sandals. Liesel helped herself to the toiletries and cosmetics that Alice had left there. Stepping out the back door, she then walked through a courtyard to where she saw Alice waiting for her at the black wrought-iron table on the patio.

The volatile oil from the leaves of the eucalyptus trees left a blue haze in the atmosphere, perfuming the air. Liesel looked around her, appreciating the beauty of her native country. Alice's back garden eased itself into bushland with views of the Blue Mountains.

Liesel was haunted by the sounds of the yellow-tailed black cockatoo, as it called for its mate, then continued defoliating a tree.

As a musician, she was always aware of the sounds of nature. From a young age, her mother had taught her to listen. 'Can you hear that?' she would ask about the hooting owl. 'Can you hear this?' she whispered as the wind rustled through the dry grass. Her mother, Liesel realised, was her first music teacher. What would her mother advise her to do? If only she had a mother! In that moment it was as if her heart was crushed, like rose petals under steel boots, as she recalled her beautiful mother's face, and how important she'd been in her childhood.

'Gorgeous morning, isn't it?' Alice asked, her voice warm and friendly, but she soon caught the apprehension in Liesel's eyes. 'Are you okay?'

'Bad dream, or something, I guess. A nightmare. I can't remember it fully.'

'Would you like to talk about it?' Alice's caring, maternal voice caught Liesel off guard, and within seconds she was crying. Alice's arms were around her straight away; rocking, consoling. 'Just let it all out. Whatever it is, let it out dear. Tears are better out than in. Trust me.'

It was a good half hour later, when Liesel finally gathered herself together. 'I am so sorry. I feel like an idiot. I don't know what came over me.'

'Are you ready to talk now?'

'Alice, honestly? I don't even know where to start. I was crying over a thousand things, some small, some huge.'

'Start at the very beginning.'

'There's a song in that!' and they both laughed.

Alice handed her a plate with an almond croissant, and poured coffee from the cafetiere. There was freshly squeezed orange juice in a glass pitcher, and a platter of tropical fruits, cut into bite-sized pieces.

'The beginning…well, I grew up in Sydney, and had the perfect parents. They adored me, as if I was the best thing that ever happened in their lives. They were so happy together.'

Liesel shared every major event of her life right up to the present day. 'I am so desperately in love with Isaac,' she said, looking up at Alice. 'I can't bear to lose someone else that I love.'

'Thank you for sharing all that. I can see it wasn't easy. I'm sorry you've had so much pain. No one should go through those sorts of losses.'

'I miss my parents so much. It's really hard not having them around to witness my life, and to share my pain and joy. No one ever replaces your parents, do they?'

A tear slipped from Alice's eyes.

'Oh Alice. I'm so sorry. Have you lost your parents?'

'Yes, but I also lost my child. My only child.'

'Alice.' Liesel's lips quivered; the pain of losing a child unthinkable to her.

'He's alive. He's alive and well, but he's not with me.'

'What do you mean? Was he kidnapped? Adopted?'

'No, nothing like that, but then again, perhaps he was in a way. He was stolen from my heart.'

'Alice?'

'I had a beautiful, charming, happy, delightful, kind, caring son: the light of my life. Everything to me. He was the reason I breathed. What I hadn't counted on when I got married was that my idea of raising a child would be so at odds with how my husband, and all the men in his family line, believed a child should be raised. My dream was to be a stay-at-home mother, and enjoy every second with him.'

Liesel tried to hold back her tears. What pain had this woman been through?

'My son was sent to boarding school in another country when he was just five years old. My life ended that day. It truly did. It was unbearable to me. My husband had no intention of him coming home for holidays. No, there'd be all sorts of summer schools he could attend. It would make him a man, he said. There was no room for negotiation, or for compromise. Every man in his family had been sent away to school, starting at age five. That tradition wasn't going to change just because I had a soft heart. I would never have had a child if I'd known that I'd have no real part in his upbringing.'

Liesel reached out, and touched Alice's hand. They were both crying.

'That's awful. Absolutely awful. No child should ever have to go through that, and certainly no mother. But Alice, you gave him the best five years of his childhood. In ways you can't imagine, you'll have shaped him.' Liesel breathed deeply, trying to calm herself. 'I'm so sorry, Alice.'

Liesel paused for a moment, then said 'Isaac was sent away to boarding school when he was young; his mother...' And then everything started fitting into place. All the scattered pieces of the jigsaw puzzle were linked together. Liesel felt her head spin. With dizziness threatening to destabilise her, she grabbed the edge of the table.

'Are you...oh my god. Are you Isaac's *mother*?'

It was all Alice could do to nod her head.

'Alice! Oh Alice. You have to see him. You have to make contact with him.'

'I want to. I desperately want to,' she cried, blowing her nose with a tissue. 'But I'm afraid he won't see me. I've written dozens and dozens of letters to him over the years, but they've all been returned unopened.'

'Alice, he was hurt. He hated boarding school. Isaac cried every day of his childhood. He was routinely bullied for being soft. I'm not telling you this for you to feel guilty, but for you to understand that huge wall he built around his heart. He lives in constant pain. And then his dad died...'

'I heard. Such a waste of life. He was a good man, really. Tough, and constrained by tradition, but good.'

'But you didn't go back for the funeral, or to comfort Isaac?'

'He wouldn't have wanted me there.'

'But you don't know that!'

'You're right. I don't know that.'

'He hoped you'd turn up. He thought you'd come up into the church at any time and wrap your arms around him. And then when the service was over, he thought you might be somewhere in the cemetery, perhaps standing under a Scots pine. For weeks afterwards, he thought you might visit.'

'It just felt like too huge a hurdle to overcome. I was a stranger to Isaac. What comfort could I have given him?'

'The hug of a mother. We never stop needing our mother.'

'Liesel, I too have suffered the depths of depression. I moved to America, to sunny Florida, in the hope I could relieve the black cloud over me. It didn't help. The only thing which would help me feel human again was to have my son with me. No mother should ever have to lose her child. In some ways, I often wondered if it had been easier if he'd died. I could have grieved properly, perhaps had some closure. But this loss just goes on and on. It might sound crazy, given he's a grown man now, but I'd do anything to put my arms around him. I've never stopped loving Isaac.'

'You will put your arms around him. *Tonight!* You're coming with me, and you will meet your son. If he expects me to return to Scotland with him, then he has to let down some more defences and allow you back into his heart.'

'You can't make him, Liesel.'

'Watch me!'

Alice couldn't help but chuckle at Liesel's determination. She'd been right to make contact with her, and request her for the party. They smiled at each other, as if they were both sending each other a life raft. Perhaps the future held some hope after all.

'So, how did you know that I was connected with Isaac?'

'The newspapers! They've been full of articles about your concerts, and there were photos of you together. As soon as I saw the name Isaac Heathfield, I knew. You know, he looked just the same as the last day I saw him. The same, but older. Those little curls with a mind of their own. That smile which makes you swoon. But his eyes looked deeper and more haunted than the loch.'

'The newspapers had photos of me and Isaac? Oh Duncan would have loved that! He hasn't said a word about it.'

They giggled a little.

'How do I get out of this situation, Alice? I don't want to break Duncan's heart, but I owe him. And maybe he's right; maybe I've transferred the affection I had for him onto Isaac. Maybe I don't know what I'm doing after all.'

'You don't owe anyone anything. Not now, not ever. This is your life. You're the one who has to wake up each day and face the consequences of your decisions. Don't make a choice you'll live to regret.'

'You make it sound so simple.'

'It is.'

They spent the day wandering through Alice's vineyard, and sharing more about their lives. 'So why don't you teach children, if that's what makes your heart sing?'

'Because everyone in the music scene tells me it's a waste of my talent.'

'Yes, but if it brings you joy then how can it be a waste?'

'You know what I'd really love to do?'

'What is it, my dear?'

'I've love to create an exclusive boarding school—don't cringe at that word—for child prodigies; but a boarding school where their parents lived, too. It could be that they just attended for a year or two, but have the finest musical education. It would be small and intimate, for say about six students in any given year.'

'What a beautiful dream, Liesel.'

'I haven't been able to get it out of my head. This is what I really want to do.'

'What do you need to do to make it happen?'

'Well, I'd probably do a few concert tours to earn the money first! And then I have to be clear about my future, about which man I'm going to be with…'

'I don't think there's any choice there, Liesel. You feel obligated to Duncan, but you're not in love with him. There's a world of difference.'

'Yes, but…'

'No buts' she winked, imagining what it would be like to have Liesel for a daughter-in-law, and wondering what it would be like to have her son back in her life.

Liesel spent the next hour describing her dream music school in great detail; her words painted a picture. Alice mentally noted every part of her dream.

At 8pm they arrived to Shangri La. 'Alice, you need to prepare yourself for the fact that Isaac will be harsh, possibly rude. Just remember, underneath all that gruff beats the world's most beautiful heart. He's just protecting himself. Whatever he says, if it sounds unkind, don't take it personally.'

'Liesel, it *is* personal. I broke his heart. I didn't fight for him. I let my husband dictate his family tradition.

No child ever gets over something like that. Boarding school steals a child's soul. He was five years old when he left. *Five!* He was a baby.'

'Your heart was broken, too. He's only ever looked at it from his point of view; now he needs to see what you went through, and how it's impacted on your life.'

Isaac was in the foyer reading a newspaper, and didn't see them approaching until they arrived at his table.

'Honey,' Liesel whispered. He looked up at her, beaming a smile of delight, ready to stand up and hug her, when his eyes caught sight of the woman with her. Isaac did a double take. Despite the passing of thirty years, and the addition of wrinkles, she looked, to him, as beautiful as she ever did.

'Mum?'

'Isaac. I'm so sorry.'

Liesel saw the lump rise and fall in his throat.

'What are you doing here? Liesel,' he said, turning to look at her, 'what are you doing with my... with my mother.' He struggled on the word mother.

'I performed at her home last night.'

'Home? You live in Australia? I thought you lived in America?'

'I did, for a while. I've lived here for twenty years.'

'Isaac, honey, I'm going to go up to my room. Be nice to your mother,' she winked. 'Alice, it's been an absolute joy getting to know you. Stay in touch.' The women reached out and held each other in a long, slow, rocking embrace which completely disarmed Isaac. He was all set to tell his mother to leave, but as he watched the indescribable bond between her and Liesel, he thought better of it. If Liesel was so taken by his mother, he should at least give her a few minutes of his time.

'I agreed to meet Duncan for lunch tomorrow. Perhaps we can have a quick catch up for breakfast?'

'Yes, yes of course.' His eyes were on his mother, not on Liesel. Old memories came flooding back. Nights of crying beneath his pillow in the dormitory; silent sobs so as not to draw attention from other boys and receive yet another beating. Days of fantasising about how he and his mother could run away from their lives, and be a proper mother and son. She looked, to him, every bit as beautiful as he remembered.

He delved back further in his memory—further, further, before the pain—to the sweet sound of her singing Scottish lullabies, and walking with her, hand in hand, through the heather-filled glens. There were food memories, too, like raspberry shortbread and cauliflower cheese. Pleasant memories came back in a deluge. She *had* loved him! His mother didn't want to leave him at school. Isaac remembered her crying, pleading, screaming to his father to let him stay; to defy ancestral tradition.

Liesel smiled as she walked away. Even if she chose Duncan, she felt joy that Alice and Isaac had been reunited. Of this she was certain: he would have a woman in his life who loved him.

Despite the first few minutes of discomfort, Alice and Isaac managed to navigate the pain, misunderstanding and fear which had gripped their lives. It wasn't until five in the morning, blurry eyed but hopeful, that they finished their conversation. Isaac had confided in Alice about his life as an award-winning, New York Times best-selling novelist. And in a tear-filled moment, shared his dreams for marrying Liesel, and becoming a

172

father. How was it so easy to talk to her, he wondered, when in reality she was a stranger. Even though there had been a thirty-year absence in their relationship, Isaac found he loved her deeply. Beneath the decades of pain, there still lived a little boy who thought his mother was everything.

'Time and absence don't stop someone loving another person. If the love is real, it transcends time,' Alice said.

Isaac thought he was talking about their relationship, but she wasn't.

'Let Liesel go. She loves you, Isaac. She'll come back to you, but you need to go home. Go to Scotland. Give her that freedom; a freedom that says: *I trust you*. How can she make a decision when you're staying in the hotel? Go home. I promise you she'll be there before you know it.'

'I'm terrified. I'm scared that...'

'Of course you are. It was me who left you, not her. Liesel hasn't left you and she's not going to walk away.'

'I feel like she already has.'

'Her heart isn't with Duncan. It never was. Remember, he held her hand through a dark night of the soul. That's not something she can forget. But, she needs to be able to say thank you to him, and to let him go. Their relationship was virtually platonic, and compared to the lightning sparks between you and Liesel, well...'

'She told you about that?' he asked in surprise. It was such a personal thing to share, especially with a stranger. But perhaps Liesel didn't see Alice as a stranger, but as family. That gave him a shred of hope to hang onto.

'Liesel has told me everything. And, mother to son, I'm telling you: the fastest and most effective way to have her back in your arms, without question or any lingering doubts, is to go home. Go back to your life in Scotland.'

'Mum, my life is nothing without her.'

'Go back,' she promised, holding his hand firmly. 'I think you're terrified that she's going to walk away... just like I did. But you have to know this, my son. I didn't walk away from *you*. I walked away from a life where I had no say in how to bring up my own child. I walked away from the immense pain of standing in Stoneyhill every day and only hearing the memory of your laughter. I walked away because I was haunted by what we had. Our relationship was wonderful. I know that you question that, and I have no doubt that you think I left you, but it was a life without you that I ran away from. You were a little boy. You saw it as me leaving you, and now you probably, at the deepest level, think every important woman in your life is going to leave you. Change the pattern. Change it now. Take back your life. Go back home, and carry on with what you'd normally do. Let her choose you. Let her come home to you.'

Isaac held onto his mother's words. Was she right? Was he expecting Liesel to leave him because that's all he'd ever known from women? What if he walked away and she didn't follow? His mind was racing at a thousand miles per second. So many choices. So many decisions. And yet, through it all, there was only one woman. One choice.

'And what about you?' he asked tentatively, trying to bring himself back to the present moment. 'When can I see you again? Can we see each other again? Mother?'

As she cried, she told him that for thirty years she had missed the sound of his voice, and his arms around her. Thirty long years.

'I will shift my whole life if it means you'll be part of it. Everything. Everything! Whatever it takes, Isaac. If you're prepared to forgive me, and let me into your world, then I'll be there without a moment's hesitation.'

'It sounds to me like there isn't anything to forgive,' he said, holding her hand. 'I can't pretend there isn't a lot of hurt, and that I didn't feel pain. That part of me isn't going to heal in a hurry, but what I can do is allow both of us to create new memories. If Liesel coming into my life has taught me anything, it's that life keeps moving forward. I want you in my life, mother. I want you.'

They held each other for a long time, without words to clutter the emotions.

Alice confided in him about Liesel's dreams of an exclusive music school. 'You know, if she set that up, I could be involved in the administration side. She wouldn't have time for that, but I've had years of doing this sort of work. I'm no vintner, but I have loved managing my vineyard. I'd be using similar skills. And that way we could all reach our dreams,' she assured him as they hugged.

'She wants a music school? She wants to teach?' He smiled. 'That's fantastic! I knew she was a natural with kids, but this…this is wonderful.'

Immediately, his brain started coming up with all sorts of ideas.

'See you in Scotland?' he laughed. 'You'll really come?'

'I wouldn't miss it for the world. And I want to be around when my grandchildren are born.'

'You're going back to Scotland?' Liesel asked, shock gripping her body. 'But you said I could have two weeks?' She sobbed into his embracing arms.

'You can still have two weeks. You can have two months. You can have two years to figure out if you want to be with Duncan, but I'm going back to my life. If you want to be with me, you'll know where I am. Sit down, Liesel. I need to tell you something.'

'What is it?'

'I live with a lot of guilt. It's not a healthy emotion to have. It's crippling! And demoralising! When my father drowned, I had just returned from school. I'd graduated the day before. My father hadn't come to my graduation, and I was furious. All those years in boarding school, and he couldn't be bothered to see me graduate. What was the point of all that suffering if he couldn't be proud of me? What I hadn't realised was that he'd become an alcoholic, and that the castle was in a perilous state. I found him with his foot stuck inside a broken floor board! I was so angry at him, and demanded answers. At that stage, he only had one staff member left because he'd spent all his ancestral money. We had a huge row. I was so angry. How could he do this to our ancestral home? How could he do this to his own family? He stomped out of the castle, and my last words,' Isaac stopped to breathe deeply. He turned away from her. 'My last words were: good riddance; don't come back if you're going to be…so useless!'

Isaac couldn't continue. He stared out the window for some time. Liesel didn't take over the conversation or try to change the subject. 'They were the last words I ever spoke to my father. When a tourist stumbled across his body washed up on the shores of loch, the police questioned me and Maximus for days. Maximus admitted that he'd heard me fighting with dad, and I was arrested for his murder.'

'But you didn't kill him, right? Tell me you didn't kill your own father, Isaac?' she asked apprehensively.

'No, I didn't. Not literally, anyway. I didn't even know that he and his bottle of gin had gone down to the loch. He had a son he didn't know, a son he'd never taken the time to know; a castle in disrepair; a wife whom he had loved deeply, but was nowhere to be found. He felt he had no reason to go on. I should have helped him. I could have set out some solutions instead of yelling.'

'You weren't to know that he'd take his own life.'

'No, but that doesn't take away the constant nagging inside me.'

'Isaac.'

Isaac pulled away, and turned his back to her.

'When Marylynn started drinking heavily, it was like throwing petrol on a fire. The feelings about losing my dad weren't buried deeply enough for me to deal with a live-in alcoholic. After her death, I was charged with her murder.'

'But you...'

'No, Liesel. Of course I didn't kill her. The charge was dropped fairly swiftly. Adalene had witnessed everything. At first, the police were reluctant to believe her statement. They suggested she was acting out of loyalty to me. And there's some truth in that. Adalene was the first woman in my life I truly trusted, and knew would always stand by my side. She'd give her life for me, though God knows why. It's not like I deserve her loyalty! Liesel, these events have shaped who I am. I don't want the guilt of yet another thing hanging over me. I have to know that you've given your relationship with Duncan a chance. I couldn't live with myself if I got in the way of that. This is an open airfare,' he said, passing her the ticket. 'It's up to you if you use it, and you can choose the date.'

'I can't believe you're doing this. You're walking away from me.' Isaac wanted to mop her tears as they fell. After all, he knew how terrifying it felt to be abandoned by someone you love. Suddenly everything his mother said made sense. Isaac *had* to go back to his life and had to give Liesel space, instead of being there every day and taunting her as she moved between her past and her future.

'But I love you! Doesn't that mean anything to you?'

'I know you do. I also know that deep down you have a lot of affection for Duncan, and maybe you even love him. Only you know the answer to that. If you want to be with me, I'll be there.'

'Will you wait for me?'

'For as long as it takes. I'll cover all your costs here at the hotel, and anything else you need. Take as long as you have to in order to be one-hundred-per-cent sure. If there's even the slightest doubt, then stay.'

'I can't believe you're walking away from me,' she sobbed, her body shaking.

'Go Liesel. Go to Duncan and resolve your feelings for him, one way or another.'

'Isaac, you're my whole world.'

'Honey, I'm part of your world. *Part of it.* Don't confuse what we had for everything in your life.'

'What we had? What we *had*!' Her eyes flared wide open in shock. 'What are you saying? You make it sound like we're over. Is that what you want?'

Isaac hadn't meant to say it like that, but the

damage was done. Damn his careless words.

'You're dumping me?' she gasped.

'No! That's not what I meant. Come here, honey. Liesel, I meant…'

But she was gone. Like a puff of wind, she was out of the door and she left his life as quickly as she'd come into it.

Isaac could have kicked himself. How could a few words cause such devastation? The last thing he wanted was to part on unfriendly terms. This wasn't what their goodbye was meant to look like. He loved her, damn it! Liesel was his whole world. All he wanted was the very best for her. Why couldn't she understand that? Why couldn't she acknowledge that he was letting her stay because he loved her? And then he started to doubt if there was any truth in the old proverb: *if you love something, set it free. If it comes back, it's yours. If it doesn't, it never was.*

As he packed his suitcases, he thought, perhaps, it was a good thing. Without her getting upset, they'd have been back in bed and inseparable. Liesel needed to be cross so that she could walk away. It was right that she could use this time to decide what was more important to her: her past or her present. Who would she take into her future?

Liesel cried all night long. The next morning, she couldn't face breakfast or lunch. When she met with Duncan, she still wasn't hungry.

'He's gone back to Scotland?' Duncan asked in disbelief, his body relaxing with relief. 'It's a good thing, Leez. It gives us a chance to get back on track,' he said, reaching for her hand.

'Don't touch me, Duncan. Don't!'

'I get why you fell for him, I really do. But can't you see it was just a fleeting affair? It wasn't mean to be. Love doesn't happen like that. It's built on friendship, and time. Do you think Heathfield would have sat by your bed for two years while you were numb with depression? Liesel? Do you?'

'I can't answer that. I don't know!'

'You can't answer it because you don't know him. You know me. You know what I'd do for you. I may not own a castle, or drive a posh car, or be able to whisk you off to a violin auction in Italy, let alone buy the damn instrument, but I sure as hell can do the things that matter, like sit by your side when your body is racked with pain! It doesn't take money to do that.'

Liesel didn't reply. Duncan's words seeped into her head. Maybe he was right. Perhaps there was more to love than feeling like you were struck by a bolt of lightning: literally or metaphorically!

Each day she spent time with Duncan, returning to her hotel suite at night. *Alone.* Oh how she missed Isaac's presence in the foyer, and each night she looked around hopefully for him, praying he'd changed his mind. Liesel was grateful to have kept one of his t-shirts, and each night before crying herself to sleep she'd breathe his natural body aroma deep into her being.

Liesel didn't return to Scotland at the end of two weeks. She was torn. Torn between two...*What?* She asked herself. *It's not like I'm torn between two lovers. I've never even made love with Duncan.* And she wondered if perhaps that was a path she needed to go down. Maybe she wouldn't really come to a definitive answer unless she surrendered to him fully. Liesel figured that was the missing link in this whole equation: she had to share her body with Duncan. Her heart felt heavy at the prospect. If she slept with Duncan, then she'd be betraying everything she held sacred about her relationship with Isaac. If she didn't have sex with Duncan, then how could she really know if she was giving him a proper chance?

Another four weeks passed. And with each day, she saw the man Duncan truly was. Finally, she let go of her angst and allowed him to be in her life. As one day flowed into another, she felt herself become lighter and more carefree. Liesel understood why he'd remained at her side for so long: he genuinely cared for her. There was no lightning between them, no magic spark, no sizzle when their skin touched, no dazzle, but there was consistency, stability, and security. Perhaps that was what real relationships were about. With each day away from Isaac, and no contact between them, she wondered if maybe he was right. Maybe she just needed to be here with Duncan without him around. They enjoyed spending time with each other, but kept their relationship as platonic as it had always been. The thought was never far from her mind: should I make love with Duncan?

For his part, he never attempted anything more than holding her hand, so she never volunteered anything else. The question still danced at the periphery of her mind, day in, and day out...all day long.

Isaac had returned to Stoneyhill Castle, his heart broken in two. The place felt so vast and empty, and the rooms were eerie. They felt colder than usual. Perhaps people were right. The place was haunted! For so long he denied the negative memories and stories that these walls held. At night, he heard Marylynn's voice calling through the halls. In his bed, he tossed and turned.

It was clear: he needed to fill these walls with happiness, with joy, with *Liesel*. Somehow he'd get her back here. Isaac tried not to let his imagination get too carried away. It wasn't worth the pain to think of what Duncan might be doing to...*his* Liesel.

Isaac called in contractors, and renovations began. Damn it; he was going to fight for her! Life was meaningless without Liesel by his side.

Walls were plastered, and bedrooms redecorated. Every sign of Marylynn and Isaac's father was removed from the castle. Isaac was astounded at the transformation, and wondered why he hadn't done something similar years ago. New life breathed into the ancient building, and there was only one thing missing: Liesel.

A team of designers and decorators worked day and night to create her dream music boarding school exclusively for child prodigies. Everything was going to plan apart from the fact that Isaac just wasn't sure how to bring Liesel back. She needed to come of her own accord. At nighttime, he lay in bed willing her to come home. In his imagination, his hands were on her again, and he found solace in his memories. Memories! The irony. Memories sustained him, and they haunted him.

Isaac had moments of wondering if his mother was wrong. Surely if Liesel was going to come back she'd have done so by now? Time was moving on, and it was doing so without the beautiful Liesel Eather in his life.

'It looks amazing, Isaac,' his mother said,

surveying the main music room. 'I'm so proud of you,' she gripped his hand tightly. 'She'll be so happy.'

'If she ever comes back. What if we've done all this, and she doesn't come back?'

'You have to trust her, Isaac. Trust her heart.'

They wandered through the various rooms. Family apartments were created, and the left wing of the castle was reserved as a home for Liesel, Isaac, Alice and accommodation for his staff. 'I want to see our children run around these rooms,' he said softly. 'What if she doesn't want children, or what if...'

'What if *what*?' Alice asked, watching the distress on his face.

'What if she's like Marylynn, and can't conceive?'

'Can't conceive? Marylynn couldn't have children? But, I thought... Liesel said Marylynn killed herself while she was pregnant.'

'She never heard that from me! She must have been privy to village gossip before we met. Somehow the rumour got around that she flung herself down the steps because I didn't want her baby. I wonder,' he said, his mind racing. 'I wonder if she had heard that before she drove up here that day? Well, it's not the truth!'

'And the truth is?'

'Marylynn had been to the doctor, that was true; he confirmed that she was infertile and could never become pregnant. Marylynn was distraught, obviously. She couldn't imagine a life stuck here in the middle of nowhere without children. This was the only reason she married me, and I hate to admit this, but she only moved here from Boston to be part of this dynasty. Without children, I wasn't enough for her. She told me so.'

'Isaac!' Alice cried. 'I'm so sorry. And I'm sorry I wasn't here for you. I'm sorry you had to go through this on your own. I'm just so sorry.'

'It's in the past, Mum. That's where it needs to stay. Marylynn tripped down the stairs. She was drunk. It was an accident, not suicide. Drinking was a daily occurrence over which she used her limber mouth to tell me how much she hated Stoneyhill and everything about it. She hated her life, and what it had become. She was deeply unhappy, but wasn't open to adoption or any other way of bringing children into our lives.'

'Why didn't you tell people?'

'Because it's none of their damn business. It wasn't anyone's business but ours.'

'You need to tell Liesel.'

'I will.'

184

True Love

'I love you, Duncan. I've loved you for as long as I've known you,' Liesel said as they dined by the Sydney harbour at sunset. As she held his hand, rubbing it lightly with her fingers, she said 'This past week has been incredible. I feel so relaxed and happy. I...I feel like my old self.' She laughed. 'Thanks to you. Isn't it funny how life can change so quickly?'

The restaurant was almost as intimate as the words she whispered. Liesel spoke softly and kindly; her tone so very far removed from how she initially spoke to him when her memory returned, and she was moved to see how touched Duncan was by her tenderness.

'I'm really glad I extended my stay, and that we had this time together to remember what we had. I needed that. It was important, not just for you, but for me. I might have made a decision I'd live to regret; a decision I'd always question if I hadn't have had this time. Your patience has been extraordinary. Two weeks would never have been enough for me to appreciate our relationship. The past two months have shown me what I value, and what's important to me, not to mention the direction of my dreams. Thank you for everything. You know, I was distressed when Isaac didn't return my phone calls, but now I can see it was a good thing. We needed a clean break so I could really focus on what you and I have. What you've done, Duncan, and how you've stood by me in what must have been excruciating circumstances, means the world. I'm so grateful to you. You're one hell of a man.'

When she smiled, Duncan thought as if he might explode from pleasure.

'Babe,' he said, his voice filled with relief. 'I feel like you've finally come back to me. I was beginning to wonder if it would ever happen, or if I'd lost you forever.'

Duncan's eyes lit up, and he reached over to hold her hand; and not for even a second did she flinch or try to pull away. And she didn't tell him not to say 'babe'. No, things were different now. There'd been a shift in their relationship and he couldn't have been happier. Everything was perfect. Finally, finally they could get on with their lives, and plan their wedding. His girl was back! Duncan wasn't going to waste another minute. Life was far too short for that. And if the past few months hadn't proven that love can conquer all, then nothing else ever would. Without hesitation, he pulled the small velvet box from his pocket.

Carefully, he opened it to reveal a beautiful diamond ring. It sparkled in the light. Strong and faithful, like Duncan's enduring commitment to her.

'Duncan,' she gasped. 'It's stunning, but let me finish talking. Please.'

He put the box on the table and reached for her hand.

'Leez?' Concern shrouded the happiness he'd been feeling. 'You don't like the ring? I can get another one. A sapphire, emerald, anything you want.'

Liesel couldn't help but wonder about something: diamonds have no colour of their own until they reflect the light.

'It's not the ring. I love you deeply. That's why I'm here. That's why I stayed in Australia, but the love I feel for you is of deep friendship and care. I love you like a brother. My feelings are platonic, not romantic. I went away to Europe because I was wrestling with this. I didn't know how to tell you. I thought that maybe with time away from me you might meet someone else. Maybe you'd come to realise that we didn't have what it takes to last a lifetime.'

Liesel's heart ached; she couldn't bear to see the tears filling his eyes. Duncan didn't deserve such pain, but he did deserve her honesty. 'My heart is with you, Duncan, but it can never be with you in the way you want it to be. And it's not fair to either of us if I stay.'

'But it's fair to Heathfield?'

'Isaac may well not want me back. I've been gone too long. He'll have been plagued by doubts about my love. I haven't been able to get in touch with him. We've not spoken to each other since the day he flew home. Adalene just keeps saying he's unavailable. He hasn't returned any of my phone calls. And his mother has sold her vineyard and moved away. I haven't been able to reach either of them. My decision about us isn't based on Isaac. It's based on you and I. It's about what we had, and what we don't have. I love you, Duncan. That is true. Let me go now. Let me be free. I know you love me. There's no doubt about that, but your love has to be strong enough to release me.'

Duncan sobbed openly in the restaurant, attracting the attention of the other diners. The woman he loved was right: he had no right to hold her back.

'This is the hardest thing I've ever done in my life,' he cried. 'Will you keep in touch?' he asked, when he eventually calmed down.

'Of course I will. It's a promise. It says such an enormous amount about you that you waited for me, even after you knew I'd slept with Isaac.'

187

'What it says is that I love you. I always will. You were my first love, and you'll be my last.' He sniffed into his handkerchief.

'Don't say that, Duncan. You deserve love. Good love. Don't close yourself off to that possibility. Promise me that you won't close yourself off to love.'

They collected her bags and violin from the hotel, and he drove her to the airport.

'If he doesn't want you, Leez, come back here. Stay with me. As friends! You'll always have a home here. I will never turn you away.'

Duncan hugged her in a way that he hoped would change her mind.

'You need to move on, Duncan. Even if I do come back to Australia, it will be to start a new life. I want to open a music school, and that will be my whole focus... and...' but she didn't tell him what else was on her mind because they were interrupted.

'Leez!' a familiar voice called out. Jessica and five other of Liesel's friends turned up at the departure lounge, half an hour before she was due to board.

'What are you all doing here?' Liesel cried. 'Please don't convince me to stay. My heart is with Isaac. I have to go back. I want to go back.'

'Don't be silly,' Jess laughed. 'We're here to hug you and say goodbye, and to tell you that we love you! And to say keep a room in that haunted castle for us!'

'Haunted?'

'You told us the other night. Apparently you went there because it was haunted. Some lady in the village shop told you about a hermit in the castle? You don't remember? And how his late wife threw herself off the stairs carrying their baby?'

Liesel placed her hand to her belly. 'Did I?'

It was all coming back to her. Another thread in her memory. Yes, she went to the castle because Isaac's story broke her heart. She wanted to mend him. 'She was expecting their baby? Isaac's wife was having a baby?'

'That's what you told us!' Jess laughed. 'Get your hand off your belly. I know you've put on weight from all that gourmet five-star hotel food, but if you don't mind me saying, you look a bit pregnant yourself.'

'No one can look a *bit* pregnant, Jess,' she laughed. 'You either are or you aren't.'

'Oh my god! Are you?'

Six pairs of arms swooped around her, joyous hoots echoing across the departure hall.

Duncan stood back. This was it, now. Time to say goodbye. His heart crashed to the floor. Liesel was not his to keep; only hers to let go. Now that he knew she was having Isaac's baby, any faint hope he'd had that she wouldn't board the plane disappeared at the speed of lightning.

'I love all of you, and of course you're welcome to visit anytime.'

Tears slipped down her face, with the tailwind of hormones pushing them into public view. She looked back at them all: *her past*. As she stood in the present, she collected a lifetime of memories and placed them tenderly in her heart, knowing they would comfort, nourish and humour her through the years ahead: *her future*.

As she boarded the plane, and made herself comfortable, Liesel gave silent thanks that Isaac had purchased a seat in first class. Right now, she needed some nurturing and care: She was between homes, between countries, between her past and her future.

What if Isaac had moved on? What if he turned her away? It was a risk she had to take, and besides, she had a gaggle of friends who would welcome her, and her baby, back with open arms if he turned her away.

For the duration of the flight, she drifted in and out of sleep, dreaming of a blonde girl who kept dancing around the castle. She was there, close, but just out of reach, laughing. When the stewardess came by with meals, Liesel held a hand over her mouth and the other hand indicated that the food needed to be taken away.

Recognising the signs, the stewardess returned with water and plain crackers. 'These will help,' she smiled, bringing a sachet of lavender for her to breathe whenever she felt nauseous.

When the Cat's Away

Liesel bristled against the cool breeze as she stepped off the plane at Edinburgh airport. For a nanosecond she wondered if she was making a mistake exchanging the warmth of the Australian Autumn for a chilly Scottish Spring. Just for a second!

A limousine was waiting for her. The driver held up a card with her name on it. *He knows I'm coming back home*, she thought to herself. *He's waiting for me.*

She knew Adalene would keep him informed, and silently gave thanks.

When they eventually drove up the hill towards Stoneyhill Castle, Liesel asked the driver to stop by the fallen tree. It had been moved to one side when she was last in Scotland, but was still there by the road: a symbol of their love; their destiny. She urged him to drive up to the castle and leave her belongings at the front door. Liesel wanted to sit awhile by the tree.

Her heart swelled at the memories they shared in the castle, and then she thought of Marylynn, and the baby. And of the baby now growing in her womb. *Their* baby. Would Isaac be happy? What would it mean for their relationship?

Eventually her heart could take it no more: she had to see him. Liesel waved at the driver as he drove by on his way back down the hill.

Knocking on the front door, she was greeted by Adalene. 'Hello Liesel. Welcome back home.' And just those words had her crying.

'There, there, dear. You'll be okay. Everything will be okay now. Maximus has taken your baggage upstairs. Come, and I'll get you some tea.'

'Where's Isaac?'

'He's out. Away on business. He said to make yourself at home.'

'He's not here?' she asked, devastated that she'd just travelled from the other side of the world to be with him. Tired, jet-lagged, and miserable, she asked 'He didn't want to be here when I got back?'

'It was urgent business. He had to attend to it without delay.'

The maid prepared tea. 'There have been a few changes since you've been gone. Isaac suggested you take a look around. I'll escort you if you like.'

'What changes?'

'A spot of decorating here and there.'

'Has he sorted out some heating?'

They both laughed. 'I think you'll find everything in good working order.'

Adalene defied etiquette, and sat down with Liesel and had a cup of tea.

'He's been pretty miserable without you here. It was touch and go for a while.'

'What do you mean?'

'We thought he might sell up and move to Australia. He said he couldn't live without you.'

'Then why isn't he here?' Liesel frowned, then wiped a tear from her cheek. She missed him so much, and he wasn't even here to welcome her.

Adalene avoided the question and said, 'Come on, have a look around. Isaac wants to be sure you approve.'

They walked from one end of the castle to the other, taking in each room. 'He's made me a music school?' She was dumbfounded.

'Do you like it?' The maid was keen for Liesel to approve.

'It's beautiful. Absolutely beautiful. It's like he

was in my mind. I don't understand how he could have seen my vision so clearly. I never told him about all the things I wanted, but here they are. How is this even possible?'

Liesel hesitated before they walked into Marylynn's room, and held her breath as she entered. It was unrecognisable. Not a hint of her or her life remained. It was a state-of-the-art recording studio. Liesel sat down on the floorboards, shaking.

'Liesel, are you okay?' Adalene sat down beside her. 'What can I do for you? What do you need?'

'Nothing. I just…I just need time.'

Eventually she stood up, walking around the vast room and surveying all the recording facilities. They were first class. 'He left this room intact for ten years.'

'Yes dear.'

'And now it's gone.'

'Yes dear.'

'But why? Why now? I just assumed he'd keep this as a shrine to her forever. That she'd always be a shadow just a few steps behind us.'

'It was never a shrine! He felt guilty, but he wasn't devoted to her. He cared for her. She was a lovely lady, but…but he didn't love her. What he feels for you, it's life-changing. Look around you. This isn't about having money to throw around. This is his statement to *you*. His declaration of undying love.'

'What happened to Marylynn's possessions?' Liesel asked, a melancholic tone teasing her throat.

'I took them to Glasgow and donated them to a women's refuge. They've gone to a good place. Her life wasn't in vain. If nothing else, it showed Isaac what he did want in a relationship.'

'I hope her life was worth more than that!' Tears

stung her eyes. She may have felt guilt at being jealous, but she also felt empathy; the woman had carried Isaac's baby!

'If you ask me, that tree didn't come down in lightning by itself.'

'What do you mean?'

'I don't know…a few seconds later, and it would have missed you. I just don't believe it happened by chance. It was fate. It was your destiny to meet Isaac. If I was of a different mindset, I'd say Marylynn had a part in bringing you together.'

Liesel dismissed the thought.

'Do you mind if I look around the rooms again?' she asked Adalene.

'Of course not. I need to get back to work. Are you okay on your own?'

'Yes, thank you.'

Liesel walked silently from room to room. Her body tingled. The apartments were self-contained, just as she imagined they'd be, and there was a communal dining hall for weekly shared meals. Several rooms were designed as teaching studios. She kept shaking her head in disbelief. How could he have known what she wanted in her music school? Even down to the colour of the walls; he seemed to have identified every desire.

Liesel headed to the wing that would be their home. Firstly, she went to the bathroom. She smiled to see it hadn't changed one bit. Everything was just as she remembered, right down to the shampoo bottle. The bedroom, too, was just the same. Liesel felt gratitude that he didn't redecorate them. This was part of her past now, and one she wanted to bring into her future.

Liesel rested on the bed, her hand touching her belly. Their baby was growing inside. She'd need help with the school. After all, she couldn't work here full-time and mother their child. She wondered if Isaac would have gone to all this effort if he knew there was a baby in the picture. And there was no way on God's Earth that any child of theirs was going to be sent away to boarding school. Even if he decided he didn't want to have a relationship with Liesel—because she'd been away too long—there was no way he'd agree to his child going away.

Liesel thought of a strike of lightning, and how the forks all reach out and touch a place of their own, yet they're all connected to the spark of light which begins out of sight beyond the clouds. As she closed her eyes, she imagined forks of light stretching out from her, reaching towards the right people to teach in her school. Two people immediately came to mind. She laughed it off. Impossible. Jack and Vissimo would never move to the Highlands to be part of her "small" venture. It was a nice dream, but she had to let it go. Then her thoughts turned to Hatti, the little girl from Eumundi in Queensland. Liesel had been immediately taken with her flair and passion, and how that girl was like sunshine. Hatti deserved to shine; to be seen. Without another thought, Liesel decided to offer Hatti a two-year scholarship, all expenses paid. If she agreed, Hatti would be her first pupil. But first she had to know if Isaac still wanted her. Her, and their baby. Liesel imagined them, years from now, walking through the castle gardens: laughing, playing, happy.

Deep in thought, she was smiling at her daydreams when she heard the door creak open.

'Isaac!' She jumped off the bed and straight into his arms. 'Tell me you still want me!'

'Isn't it obvious?'

'Tell me anyway! Tell me a thousand times. Tell me every single day. Tell me for the rest of my life! I will never tire of hearing you tell me that you want me, or that you love me.'

'I love you, Liesel Eather. I will always love you. I fell in love with you on the day we met, even though you infuriated me by driving onto private property. I was in love with you before you even opened your eyes. I will never stop loving you. I'm going to love you forever.' They enjoyed a long, slow, rocking hug. 'You came back,' he said, breathing a sigh of relief. 'You came back to me.'

'I was never gone. Not really. You were always in my heart. Nothing could keep us apart. I loved Duncan. I really loved him. I still do,' she said, looking down at the floor. 'I loved him as a friend, though, and that's why I had to stay as long as I did. I needed to reconcile my feelings, my gratitude...'

'Shhh. I know. I know.'

'I choose you. I didn't know who I was when I met you, but that is what made this love so strong. It wasn't based on having things in common or about our lives fitting together. I loved you, and you loved me, even when I didn't know who I was. We fell in love when I was my true self rather than someone who was moulded and shaped by other people.'

Isaac kissed her on the lips, slowly at first, and then hunger began to build. 'We've got company for dinner, but first I need to satisfy my appetite. I'm starving for you,' he growled softly, removing her blouse. When his lips moved from hers, down the nape of her neck, she sighed. Unclasping her bra, he let out a deep moan as excitement shivered across his skin. 'I'm a hungry man, Liesel. I hope you're ready for me!'

It was as if he was praying before a sacred altar: his touch was devotional. Taut muscles leaned into her, his body smelling of sweet, warm spicy cumin, and her own hunger growled in the pit of her belly.

'Isaac…'

'Don't say anything. You're here now, that's all that matters. Let me make love to you,' and he kissed his way across her breasts. Isaac wanted Liesel to cry out for him, to reach the point where she couldn't survive another moment without him inside her. That moment was almost there. He could see it in her eyes. Lightning struck. This was it. That moment of power, when they would join together.

Isaac Heathfield was home. He'd waited so long to reconnect with her again, and now, with each movement, he tipped her further and further away from memories of her past, and tilted her towards their future. *Their* future.

Liesel cried out in ecstasy, and she cried tears. 'They're tears of happiness,' she assured him.

Tears fell from his eyes, too. If ever there was a place to cry, to let your guard down, it was when making love. Those moments of surrender, that release into the other person.

'You're so beautiful to me, Liesel.' His voice was soft and low.

They rounded the hilltop of their pleasure, crying out into the late afternoon. Intense bliss coursed through their veins, and their bodies pulsed with ecstasy. Isaac filled her physically and emotionally. They climaxed together, not aware of anything else in the world but how they felt in each other's arms. He breathed her into his soul, the sweet scent of arousal and contentment all-consuming. 'You smell so good to me.' Isaac groaned, as their heads shared a pillow. 'I want to breathe you in every day for the rest of my life.'

Liesel smiled at him, her fingers tracing his strong jawline. 'I love you more than you'll ever know. It would be impossible to love anyone more.'

They lay in each other's arms, gently stroking each other's skin. It didn't seem like more than half an hour had passed, when Isaac wanted to make love to her again. He was kissing her belly, savouring her soft curves, and the gentle natural padding of flesh, less firm than it was when they were first together, when he looked up at her and caught her eyes. *A spark!*

'Are you...Liesel,' he gulped, feeling a strange sense of vertigo, as if he might lose his balance: 'Are you pregnant?'

'Yes, Isaac. I'm having our baby.'

In an instant, he laughed and lifted her up into his arms. 'We're having a baby?'

She laughed with him. 'Yes. You're going to be a father.' Liesel giggled at his incredulity.

He probably said 'We're having a baby!' no less than thirty times in the next half hour. 'Shut up, Isaac, and make love to me again. We've got years of sleep deprivation and broken nights ahead of us. Let's honeymoon while we can.'

He figured that they might be interrupted from daily lovemaking for a year or two, but he had a whole lifetime of loving ahead of him.

As they climbed the mountain of ecstasy, urging each other higher and higher, then collapsing into a dizzy descent, Isaac caught a flash of the title of his next novel: *Touched by Lightning*. It would be a passionate love story based on the theme of thunder snow and destiny.

They fell asleep for an hour or so, nestled in each other's arms. When they awoke, Isaac looked searchingly into her eyes. 'We're really having a baby?'

'Yes, honey, we are.'

If ever she had any doubts about their relationship or about impending parenthood, they evaporated in his smile. They were made for each other, and nothing would ever get in the way of that again.

Isaac glanced at the bedside clock. 'We've got visitors coming in half an hour. We better get ready for dinner.'

'Who's coming?' she asked.

'It's a surprise,' he said, leading her to the bathroom. 'Come and share a shower with me. Water's rare in Scotland. Best if we conserve it.'

Liesel giggled as he hauled her into his arms, and pulled the shower curtain in an attempt to hide them from the world. As Isaac made love to Liesel for the third time that afternoon, it occurred to him that he could give up his career as a writer, and devote himself to loving her full time. It would be a perfect way to spend the rest of his life.

'So you think making love to me three times in one day is enough when we've been apart for so long?' she teased as she sought out a dress for the evening. 'I thought you might have tempted me with Beethoven's fifth! They just don't make castle owners like they used to!'

Isaac marvelled at her lightness. It was so good to have her back here, back in his life, back in his arms.

'I'm sure we could arrange it. The night is young. What's your preference, my love? The slow movement or the fast?' He wrestled her to the bed, tickling her into submission. Dinner would have to wait!

Liesel dressed simply in an elegant forest-green linen dress, and Isaac wore an Italian suit. 'I feel a little underdressed,' she complained.

'You look perfect,' he whispered. 'Just perfect. And besides, I'm quite partial to you being underdressed!'

Isaac held her hand, never feeling more proud in his life, and they walked to the large dining room off the kitchen. Liesel could hear voices, and laughter filtering through the hallway.

As they entered the room, her hand went straight to her mouth, a failed attempt to stop a scream of joy erupting. 'Alice! Jack, Vissimo! What are you all doing here? Isaac?' she asked, 'how did you get them all here?'

'Vissimo and Jack are your additional violin tutors, and Alice will be in charge of all administration and the day-to-day running of your school. If you have any complaints or questions, then see me,' Isaac laughed.

Liesel shook her head in utter disbelief. 'This isn't real. This can't be possible. Isaac, you did this for me?'

'We all did this for you. Are you happy?'

She couldn't speak. Her eyes searched his.

'Are *you* happy?' she asked him. 'Isaac, are you happy? Is this what you want?'

'I want you. I only want you. And I want what will make you happy.'

With each passing day, Liesel felt her heart grow as big as her belly. Life felt full and rich. Her present and her future couldn't have been more different to her past, and yet they were both connected, tied by a flash of lightning.

Six children were booked into the Stoneyhill School for Violinists, and preparations were being made for the start of the school year in September. The families arrived during the last month of Summer so they could settle in to their new environment, and get to know the local area.

Liesel found Alice to be a wonderful friend and surrogate mother. Their laughter often caught Isaac in the pit of his belly, and he pinched himself. *It's real, Heathfield. It's real!*

Conversations revolved around the boarding school's menu and whether or not to include tartan in her wedding dress.

'Have you ladies still not figured that out?' Isaac laughed when he entered the kitchen. 'Perhaps you could have thistle on one side of your head, and a bunch of gum nuts on the other side,' he offered, laughing at the thought of it. He pinched a piece of Scottish raspberry shortbread off the cooling rack.

'Hey! They're still cooling!' Liesel said, rapping his fingers with a wooden spoon.

'Mum, they taste as good as I remembered. Thank you!'

Alice smiled, and said 'Liesel made them. But just to set the record straight, she's already eaten five!'

Isaac grabbed a handful. 'We're even, now,' he chuckled.

Alice was gathering ingredients to show Liesel her secret Arran potato salad: red beets, frozen peas, waxy potatoes, fresh parsley, onion, seasoning and salad cream.

'Children love the way it goes pink,' Alice promised her. 'Make sure Adalene includes it on the menu.'

They spent the afternoon bottling Scottish wild apple and ginger chutney. 'That should get us through the next year,' Alice said, putting the last of the labels on re-used glass jars. 'Sure feels good to be in this kitchen again; back here with my son.'

'This is rather fun. I used to cook all the time with my best friend Jess,' Liesel said. 'We had curry nights, pancake breakfasts. Our home always had some musician friend coming through wanting a free feed!' she laughed.

'Get that Gaelic soda bread from the oven now, and then I'll show you the meal Isaac loved when he was a little boy.' Alice had a smile on her lips. 'Adalene has tried to make it, apparently', she said quietly in case the maid overheard her, 'but Isaac said it's not like how he remembers it. Let's give him a surprise.'

Alice gathered together roughly chopped mushrooms and a dozen green peppers, heavy-cream, cauliflower, sharp-cheddar cheese and oatmeal. 'It's cauliflower cheese, but the secret ingredient is whisky! It needs six tablespoons,' Alice said without batting an eyelid.

'You gave your baby boy whisky?' Liesel feigned horror.

'Trust me, once you've tried this, your own kids will be eating it!' Alice laughed. 'And boy will they sleep well at night,' she hooted.

Liesel spontaneously hugged her. 'I love you, Alice Heathfield.'

Two nights later, Liesel, Isaac, Alice, Jack, Vissimo, the castle staff, and the six new families in residence, dined at the local pub. Liesel was excited about the curriculum, and how they'd meet the children's educational needs, personally and within the group. Two tutors would offer lessons in mainstream subjects, such as English, maths, science, drama and history; and more-relaxed classes, such as learning about native plants, and studying Gaelic folklore, would be incorporated. The vast majority of the day would be devoted to violin. Liesel was excited to say that Italy's premier violin maker would be teaching them on their very first day. She said it was important to understand their instruments, and exactly why they make the sounds they do.

The pub was the heart of their Highland community, and the townsfolk were friendly. After a few ales too many, Isaac stood up and tapped on his glass to gather everyone's attention. A stillness descended over the crowd. He decided that the ten-year rumour about Marylynn's death should come to an end, and then he expressed his absolute joy at impending fatherhood, and invited the locals to join him and Liesel for their wedding the following month. Cheers went up, and drinks were bought all round.

'Isaac Heathfield, your dad would be proud of you!' came the voice of an elderly man in the corner of the pub. 'Real proud of you, son.'

Isaac nodded in gratitude, blinking back a feral tear as he caught his mother's eyes. He hoped the man's words were true.

The atmosphere in the pub was cosy, and despite being decorated with tartan, Liesel still couldn't decide if she wanted it in her wedding. It felt alien to her.

Traditional foods were served, and Isaac treated his guests to a boutique whisky. He offered Liesel an apple juice.

'You obviously don't know what goes into your cauliflower cheese,' Liesel laughed, shaking her head, 'if you think our baby hasn't been imbibing alcohol!'

The night was memorable, and Isaac hoped these families, which had come from all over the globe, would feel that they were able to join in the local community in a way that he hadn't ever done before.

There's a Storm Brewing

Under the light of a waning moon, the clock hands sat at 3 and 12.

'3am?' Isaac said, when the phone tore him abruptly from slumber. '3am?' He walked into the hallway and lifted the receiver. 'Stoneyhill.'

'Is Liesel there?'

'She is, but it's 3 am.'

'I'm so sorry. This is Jess. From Australia. I forgot the time difference. This is important. Can I speak to her?'

Isaac reluctantly put the phone down, and woke Liesel. He hated to disturb her. She looked so peaceful, so sweet.

'Honey. Honey, there's a phone call for you. It's Jess. She says it's important.'

'What? Jess?' Liesel sat upright in bed. 'Jess? Is she okay?'

'I don't know. Go and take the call,' he said, then wrapped his dressing gown around her to protect her from the draught in the hallway.

'Jess? What's the matter Jess?'

'Are you sitting down?'

'Yes.'

'It's Duncan. He...' Jess broke down, her sobs choking up the phone line.

'What's happened?' Liesel asked, panic overwhelming her.

'He was out on his boat and it capsized when some tourists lost control of their speedboat. He's in intensive care. Liesel, he's on life support. His mother is desperate for you to come and see him.' Jess continued 'She says he just hasn't been the same since you left, and she feels that having you here would help him to recover.'

'But Jess, I'm not with Duncan anymore. I'm here, with Isaac. It's not fair for her to even ask that of me.'

'I know that, it's just...they're not sure if he'll survive.' Jess broke down and cried, and then there was silence for a long time.

'Liesel, are you there?'

Tears softly fell down her cheeks. The man who had stood by her side during the dark night of her soul was now going through his version of hell, and where was she? On the other side of the world with the man she loved, and having his baby. Something about it just didn't seem right. Her tears turned to sobs. 'I'm so sorry this has happened. Which hospital is he in?'

Jess filled her in on all the relevant information. 'So, you're coming back then?'

'No, Jess. I'm not. I will send flowers, and I will pray night and day for his recovery. And with everything inside of me, I hope he survives and returns to excellent health. But no, I'm not coming back.'

Now it was Jess's turn for silence. It seemed incomprehensible to her that Liesel would turn her back on him. She'd spent years witnessing him as Liesel's support system.

'Jess, I'm growing a *baby*. That's where my energy has to go. Duncan wouldn't expect anything less of me. I'm sorry to disappoint you.'

'I just don't know what to tell his mother. She was adamant that you were the only thing that would bring him back to life.'

'Don't worry about Nell. I'll call her.'

Nell Trantor respected Liesel's choice, and phoned every day with a progress report. The only thing was: there was nothing to report. Day after day he remained under twenty-four-hour supervision. There was no visible damage to the brain, but no signs of recovery, either.

More than once, Liesel wondered if she'd been wrong in declining her request. She took a long walk up the hill behind the castle, claiming she needed some time on her own, and plenty of fresh air. Isaac kept an eye on her through the window of one of the turrets and hoped she wouldn't walk out of sight. It wouldn't be long till sunset, and he most certainly didn't want her out alone.

Liesel had perched on a tuft of grass, her legs crossed, yoga style, with a thick woollen shawl wrapped around her shoulders, and was looking out towards the loch.

Isaac wondered if she was meditating or praying. For a moment, he couldn't bear to see her in such an isolated position. He wanted her home, here, safe in the castle; protected by strong walls.

Isaac wasn't sure what was more inspiring: the land around him which was remote, beautiful, and isolated, or her. Both of them had stolen his soul and kept him captive. Liesel sat in the same position for over an hour, and then he noticed she tipped her head and was crying. He couldn't stand it any more! If it was that difficult to be away from Duncan during this time, then she had no choice. She had to go.

Isaac grabbed his coat and put on his boots. Liesel's needs had to come first. He'd trusted her to come back to him last time. He could trust her again.

It was getting hard to see now that the Sun had

sunk behind the hills. Why hadn't she come back earlier, while it was still light?

'Liesel?' he called. She was no longer where he had last seen her. Where had she gone? There was only one path home. Why hadn't he seen her? It wasn't that dark. Surely he couldn't have missed her!

'Liesel? Liesel?' He yelled as loudly as he could. 'Liesel?' His voice boomed in a deep echo across the valley.

'Isaac,' he heard a soft voice call out in the dark. 'I'm here. Just over here.'

He shone the torch all around. 'Keep talking so I can follow your voice. Are you okay? Are you hurt? Talk to me Liesel.'

'I'm here. I tripped, and I've hurt my ankle. I don't think I can walk.'

Isaac kept following the sound of her voice, collapsing with relief when he arrived by her feet.

'I've never been more pleased to see you in my life!'

'Really?' she laughed.

'Really!'

He felt around her ankle, unsure if it was broken or if she'd torn a ligament.

'Right, I'll carry you home. You hold the torch.'

'Isaac?'

'Yes, honey.'

'Why did you follow me up here?'

'I...I saw you crying. I,' he choked on his words. The idea of letting her travel to Australia was crippling him. But what choice did he have? If he loved her, then he had to trust that she'd return.

He sighed deeply. 'I came to tell you that you should go to Duncan.'

208

'I was crying because I couldn't bear to ever be apart from you again. I wasn't crying because I felt I should be with Duncan. I was crying because I should be with you! Me and our baby. We belong *here*. You are the love of my life.'

'No regrets?'

'Not a single one.' She kissed his cheek. 'Never a doubt.'

Isaac had spent a couple of months studying lightning, and now considered himself quite the expert in fulminology. The more he understood about electrical discharges, the more he came to appreciate how Liesel had turned up in his life without warning, knocking him out of his dark cloud. He laughed to discover that men are six times more likely to be struck by lightning than women! That only served to highlight that Liesel was meant to come into his life. The local story was that Liesel's car had been struck by lightning, that fateful night on the hill, but Isaac knew the truth: he was the one who'd been struck by lightning. Touched. He'd been *touched* by Lightning, and she'd changed his life. He marvelled at the huge changes which had taken place in his life, and he knew without doubt that none of them could have happened without her. It was like his whole world had spun on its axis, shifting everything he believed to be true.

Isaac kept looking at his watch. Where was she? This was their wedding day and Liesel was nowhere to be found. None of his staff had seen her, and Alice had no idea where she was. Had she changed her mind?

Old fears began to surface. Memories of his mother leaving him when he went to boarding school, haunted him. His late wife saying that he wasn't enough for her, kept replaying at the edges of his mind.

What if Liesel was having second thoughts? What if, now that they were close to becoming man and wife, she realised that Duncan was the man she should be marrying? Perhaps his near brush with death had been a wake-up call.

Isaac walked into the room she was using to prepare for the wedding. The dress was hanging there in a plastic protector. Why wasn't she dressed yet? Guests would be arriving soon. Panic had his heart pounding. Surely he should know by now that their love was real. Isaac was frustrated that he still didn't feel worthy of her; and that she had the power to walk away at any time. Would he be haunted by the deep residue of abandonment for the rest of his life? Even now that his mother was back living at Stoneyhill, eagerly awaiting the birth of her first grandchild? What would it take to heal the wound?

Liesel and Hatti walked, hand in hand, over the fields and hills towards the loch, giggling and whispering secrets. They talked about how she had settled into the school, and what it was like to be able to devote her days to full-time violin practice. Hatti gathered together bouquets of heather and asked 'Will you wear these in your hair? The lady in the village shop said the Scottish believe they're good luck.' It was such a simple gift from the child Liesel had chosen to be her flower girl. Simple, but meaningful.

'They're perfect.' Liesel smiled, and suggested they

head back home. The wedding was a few hours away, and it was time for them to get ready. She'd forgotten to tell Isaac that they were popping out for a few minutes. The last thing she wanted was him fretting about her. He fussed over her and her growing bump throughout the days and nights, tending to their every need.

'Are you okay?' Isaac asked when Liesel and Hatti came into the kitchen giggling.

'Perfectly okay! It's my wedding day. Can you believe it? Today I'm going to become Mrs Liesel Heathfield. Okay? I couldn't be happier!' She hugged him tightly, and said she had to get a move on. Alice would be waiting for her upstairs.

The wedding day had approached quickly. Despite feeling like she had to squeeze into her wedding dress, Liesel looked exquisite: a picture-perfect bride.

'There's a storm coming,' Alice fussed, brushing Liesel's hair and decorating it with the flowers Hatti had gathered from the hillside.

'Perfect,' Liesel smiled as she looked in the mirror. Alice thought she meant the floral crown was perfect, but Liesel's thoughts were on lightning.

Friends, family and folk from the local village began to gather at Stoneyhill Castle for the wedding about to take place in the gardens. There were familiar faces in the crowd: Jessica; Jake and his boyfriend; a rehabilitated Duncan; Jack; Vissimo; the castle staff; Hatti and the other children and parents.

Liesel watched the pewter clouds gathering on the horizon, teasing her with the promise of a storm. Her belly was full and round, and as she walked with grace across the lawns towards Isaac, her baby kicked with each rumble of thunder.

The gown was simple, yet elegant, draping in soft layers from an empire line. Ribbons of tartan from the ancestral Heathfield clan lined the hem of her gown.

Isaac wore a tuxedo, with matching tartan bow tie.

Liesel had decided against a formal arrangement of flowers, and instead chose a bouquet of wild heather.

Oak trees surrounded the celebration area. Glass lanterns, with small candles flickering inside, hung from the branches swaying gently in the breeze. Tartan ribbons were tied to the chairs. A small table served as a devotional space, with flowers, candles and the celebrant's order of service.

Liesel had argued vehemently about bagpipes at the wedding, and Isaac agreed that they weren't his thing, but that it was important to bring a Scottish feel to their ceremony. After all, this was where they met, and where they were going to raise their children. Liesel promised to do her best, and would surprise him with some Scottish music. But he surprised her first. The school children had been instructed by Liesel to play a classical piece of music as she walked towards Isaac, under the canopy of oak trees, but instead they played a medley of Scottish fiddle pieces. Liesel laughed out loud, and as she caught Isaac's smiling eyes she realised he'd put them up to it. *Oh how she loved him!* What a great team they made.

Lightning flashed in the background, and she knew all was right in the world.

Alice had her arm linked with Liesel's, and was honoured to be asked if she would give Liesel away. 'I can think of no better man for you to marry,' she laughed. 'There's no finer woman I'd want him to wed.'

'We are gathered this day...' the celebrant began, but

her words were barely audible above the rumble of thunder.

Vows were spoken as sacred words, and tears fell from Liesel's eyes as she looked up into Isaac's face. His eyes no longer held the look of the haunted loch, but were bright, clear and penetrated her soul. They'd found each other.

Lightning lit up the sky. There were several readings, poems and songs which served as a testament to the holy path of love. Liesel could have stayed out there all day, but when the ceremony ended, she encouraged her guests to head indoors before the rain fell.

The children scattered white and purple heather blossoms before Isaac and Liesel as they walked together, as man and wife, into the great dining hall for the celebrations.

The guests were seated in the beautiful reception area, which was decorated in Heathfield tartan and aboriginal art. Bouquets of baby-blue eucalyptus leaves, banksia, kangaroo paw and other native Australian flowers had been chosen, and were arranged in between vases of heather and purple thistle. Liesel insisted that they blend their cultures. It was important, she said, that their children would know both the past and the future. Surprisingly, they didn't clash nearly as much as Isaac supposed they would.

Isaac and Liesel arrived at the bridal table to Jack and Vissimo playing their violins. In all her childhood daydreams of getting married, and being a princess bride, nothing surpassed the reality of her wedding day: a music teacher marrying a writer.

When Isaac made his toast, he looked into his wife's eyes. 'Mrs Heathfield, you struck my life like lightning, changing my path without warning, and every single day you make me desire you like the rumble of thunder tearing through the base of my being until I can't think of anything else but you, and only you; but more than that,' he said thoughtfully, 'you fill my life with sunshine. No matter where we travel to, or what comes our way, you are the whole world to me.'

Five Years Later

The young girl, with long blonde braids, skipped across the castle gardens several metres ahead of her parents; her cats Beethoven and Grammar scampering alongside her. Storm clouds brewed above the oak trees, and the first spots of rain descended from the heavens.

'Mama, mama! Come quick! Lightning is in the sky. I *love* lightning. It's so exciting. I could just dance here all day long.' A shiver of excitement ran up the young girl's body as she was transformed by the electricity in the air.

If they ever had any doubt about the unusual name they had chosen for her, they didn't now: *Ashani*, Hindu for lightning.

Isaac squeezed his wife's hand gently, admiring her growing belly. Liesel was eight months pregnant with their second child.

'Like mother, like daughter,' Isaac laughed. They continued their discussion on baby names.

'If we were a normal couple we'd choose Heather or Glen or something appropriate for this part of the world,' Liesel laughed.

'Yes, but there's nothing normal about us!' Isaac said.

'Mama, Papa, I know just the name! I know! I know! The lightning flash told me,' Ashani said, her excitement causing her to tip her dainty little head from side to side.

'Let's call him Storm!'

'A *Scottish* Storm? That'd be a first!' Isaac said.

'I love it!' Liesel agreed, kissing her daughter on the cheek. 'We'll call him Storm.'

'*If* it's a boy!' Isaac said, having the last word.

~ **The End** ~

Novels by Veronika Robinson

Mosaic
Bluey's Café

The Gypsy Moon Trilogy
Sisters of the Silver Moon
Behind Closed Doors
Flowers in Her Hair

Sweet Cinnamon Romance
Love at the Treble Clef Café
Love in a Scottish Storm
On the Wings of Love
Recipe for Love
House of Hearts

Moonlight and Motif
(magical realism novels publishing in 2023)
The Button Tin
The Soapmaker
The Irish Dollmaker

For a list of the author's non-fiction titles, visit
www.veronikarobinson.com

About the Artist: Heidi Harbers

Happiest when she's brightening up the world, whether it's decorating a room, painting a mural, growing a garden, feeding her chickens avocados, or organising fun events in her village, creativity is at the heart of Heidi's life.

As a pub landlady, and former restaurant owner, she has cooked for thousands of people across the years, serving up delicious meals, both traditional and unusual. When not cooking, Heidi's flare for transforming bare walls into canvases for her community to enjoy has earned her a wonderful reputation.

Australian born and raised, Heidi has travelled the world; and for many years has called England home. Born under the zodiac sign of Libra, the lovers, it is only natural that her art has found a home on the covers of romance novels.

Review Me

As an indie author, it would mean the world to me if you left a review of this book on Amazon or your chosen online bookstore. Thank you so much! ~ Veronika

Sweet Cinnamon
Romance